Mary Elizabeth Raines

CW00660314

The Secret of Eating
Raspberries

The Secret of Eating Raspberries
Copyright © 2018 by Mary Elizabeth Raines

Cover design by Mary Elizabeth Raines
Illustrations by Mary Elizabeth Raines

Published by
Laughing Cherub Unlimited
Sedona, AZ 86336
www.books-plays-scripts.com

ISBN: 978-0-9726146-5-8
Printed in the United States of America

THE SECRET OF EATING RASPBERRIES

by

MARY ELIZABETH RAINES

*Dedicated to all people who manage to learn to like
one another, despite their differences.*

Mary Elizabeth Raines
Sedona, Arizona

TABLE OF CONTENTS

i

CHAPTER ONE
Riding Her Bicycle to Her New Summer Job
❦

THE FIRST MORNING

S HE HEARD THE battered pickup truck long before she saw it. The pavement beneath her bicycle began to shake with loud thumps from the truck's subwoofer, and the blast of music soon drowned out the gentle Debussy prelude she had been listening to.

Staying carefully in the bike lane, Ginny slowed and reached up with one hand to adjust her earbuds in a fruitless attempt to block out the sounds. As the pickup approached, it swerved across the white line and came dangerously near to her bicycle, throwing her off balance. The inattentive driver, red-haired and freckle-faced, was busy draining a can of beer, his head tipped back. Sprawled casually in the truck's open cargo bed were two men and a woman. They seemed oblivious to the deafening racket. As

Ginny struggled to keep her bike from falling over, the trio whooped gleefully.

One of them, a gangly young man, hollered over the booming music to the driver, "Hey, Dick, you shit-head, you missed! Ain't you drunk enough yet?"

The female, who was leaning up against him, yelled happily, "Get off the road, bitch!"

Their companion raised his middle finger and glared sullenly at the bicyclist.

Shaken, Ginny pulled off onto the grass to regain her composure. As the truck lurched away, she saw a bright green bumper sticker on the left rear fender boasting the cheerful proclamation *Support Your Local Parks*. On the opposite side was another bumper sticker, lopsided and so faded that it was nearly illegible. It said *Eat Shit, Retard*.

Picking up speed, the driver of the truck tossed his empty beer can out the window. The thuds of the music gradually diminished, leaving the discarded can to roll helplessly back and forth in the middle of the road until it was flattened by oncoming traffic.

After a few moments of deep breathing, Ginny tightened her helmet, got back on the bicycle, and continued on the way to her new summer job, her good mood deflated.

CHAPTER TWO
Honeybees and Summer Plans
❦

SEVERAL DAYS EARLIER

T HE HONEYBEE BUZZED in frustration, crawling back and forth across the window in a vain attempt to reach the outdoors. Suddenly a drinking glass was clapped over the bee. A piece of sheet music slid under the rim, trapping it in the glass.

"Gotcha!" cried Ginny.

She moved the covered glass quickly to a lower casement that had been cranked open and released the bee, who flew dizzily into the afternoon sunshine.

Ginny put the empty glass on top of the piano and returned to the doorway of her classroom where two of her fellow teachers stood ready to resume the conversation that had been interrupted by the bee. It was the final day of school. Piles of well-worn songbooks were stacked high on the piano bench, with empty cardboard boxes on the floor beneath them waited to be filled. In the hallway behind the teachers a noisy stream of schoolchildren headed jubilantly home for the summer, their backpacks and arms bulging with the remnants of the projects and papers they had cleaned from their desks. Used to ignoring the high-pitched clamor, the teachers continued their conversation.

"Okay, so where was I?" said Ginny.

Ginny was a sweet-faced white woman, a little bit plump, who was dressed respectably in a blue blouse tucked neatly into black slacks. Her graying brown hair was cut in a bob, and she had a short nose and fair skin. She looked exactly as one might imagine an elementary-school music teacher should look, replete with a pair of reading glasses fastened to a chain that hung around her neck. The only feature that stood out on her otherwise ordinary face was her smile. It was small, but bright and dimpled. Ginny smiled a lot. It made people trust her, and they were right to do so.

Leaning on either side of the doorframe were her closest friends, Tracy, a stocky blonde whose sharp, inquisitive eyes missed no detail, and Beth, a fast-talking woman with frizzy dark hair pulled up into an unkempt bun. Both of them were taller than Ginny and hovered above her. The three had known one another for a long time.

"You were telling us about the spring concert," said Tracy.

"Oh, right. The spring concert. So there they are, all my kids lined up on stage, it's the big finale, and I'm conducting my heart out when suddenly I hear this horrible sound," said Ginny. "Wouldn't you know, that awful noise is coming from little Joey Sullivan."

"Who else," said Tracy.

Beth nodded in understanding. All the teachers knew the pint-sized second-grader with his gap-toothed grin and impish giggle.

"He's in the first row," said Ginny, "and he's singing at the top of his lungs, belting it out. Off-key. Seriously off-key. I mean, he was singing four notes lower than anybody else. So I give him a stage-whisper and say, '*Joey! Higher! Higher!*' You'll never guess what he does. He goes through the whole rest of the concert like this!" Ginny rose up on her tiptoes and wobbled awkwardly. "Still singing four notes too low, of course!"

Beth and Tracy laughed, and then stepped back as a little girl with a pink backpack brushed past them and rushed into the room, her pigtails bouncing. She threw her arms exuberantly around Ginny's waist.

"Goodbye, Ms. Lawson," squealed the girl. "You're my most favorite teacher in the whole wide world!"

Ginny crouched tenderly down to the level of the child, who continued to cling to her. "Gee, Stephanie, thank you," she said. "I like you a lot, too."

Stephanie kept her warm sticky hands clasped around the teacher. After a few moments, Ginny tactfully peeled off the little girl and stood. "Hurry up now so you don't miss the bus. I'll see you in music class next year."

Stephanie turned with a giggle and ran away. Ginny called after her, "Keep singing! And have fun this summer!"

The hug ignited a glow inside Ginny. Children made her happy. She loved their open minds, their squeaky voices, their candor, and their wild enthusiasm. She even liked the way they smelled, a musky mixture of playground dirt, sneakers, and tomato soup. The children sensed her affection and loved her back.

Ginny had a warmth and friendliness that made her popular with her fellow teachers as well.

"I remember that concert," Tracy said. "How many Sullivan kids are there, anyway?"

"Have to be at least thirty-two of 'em, because that's how many years I've been teaching here, and I swear to God I've had a Sullivan in my class every year," replied Beth. "Well, kiddos, time for me to mosey on back to my room and finish packing up my class. Summer vacation beckons!" Despite her suggestion, she failed to move.

"What are you going to do this summer?" Ginny asked. "Planned anything special?"

"Oh, you bet," answered Beth. She glanced over her shoulder to make sure that no children were within earshot, and then turned back, speaking in a more subdued tone of voice. "First I'm going to work in my garden. Next, I'm going to paint my living room. And *then* I'm going to buy my husband a thong and let him bring me margaritas while I sit in a lawn chair and read trashy romance novels."

"Hey, I like that!" cried Tracy. "Maybe I'll spend my summer doing the same thing. Well, all except for the gardening part. And the painting part."

Ginny laughed.

"What about you, Ginny?" said Beth.

"Sure, I'm in. What kind of schedule does your husband have?"

"I meant what are you doing with your summer, you wanton hussy! Just you forget about the margaritas. No divorcee's gonna get her hooks into my fellow," teased Beth.

Ginny had been married for a brief time when she was in her early 20s. Her husband, a man she had only known for a few weeks, had been charming but immature. Their impulsive union had ended after only two months in an uncontested divorce.

"Your Jim is perfectly safe," she said with a rueful smile. "Even if he weren't, it's been so long, I don't think I'd even remember what to do."

"Well, okay, so now that we know what you *won't* be doing this summer, what *are* you going to do?" asked Beth.

"Believe it or not, I got myself a job with the City Parks Department. I'm going to be teaching arts and recreation—you know, for that new kids' day camp program," replied Ginny.

"Let me see if I'm hearing you correctly," said Beth. "You, the Lincoln Elementary School music teacher, are spending your vacation from teaching by *teaching*?"

"I love to teach," protested Ginny. "I really do. And I really love the kids, too...."

"And she really needs the money," interjected Tracy.

"And I really need the money," echoed Ginny, covering up her discomfort with that thought by walking over to her piano and loading a stack of books into one of the boxes.

This past spring she'd had to buy a new car, and at the same time she had gotten slammed with dental bills that her insurance didn't cover. She desperately needed to continue working over the summer to get back on her feet. The opportunity to work at a job that she would actually enjoy had come as a huge relief, and she was excited.

"When do you start?" said Beth.

"Would you believe Monday? I can't wait!"

The City Parks Department had not only accepted her application; they had sent a notice saying that they wanted her to begin working right away, which meant an immediate paycheck. It couldn't have fallen into place more perfectly. The building where she had been assigned to teach arts and recreation was less than two miles from her home, which meant that she could ride her bike to work.

CHAPTER THREE
The New Job

MONDAY

THE SIGN CLEARLY said *Building 5, City Parks Service*. Ginny stood astride her bicycle, staring at it doubtfully. Behind the sign was a hut partially built into a hill that appeared to be more of a hard-worn shed than an arts and crafts building. She had expected to see a sizable parking lot nearby for the busy traffic of parents who would be dropping off their kids, together with picnic tables and a playground. Instead, there were only a few parking spaces adjacent to the dingy structure. A truck occupied one of them. The shed stood next to a fenced lot filled with large yellow construction vehicles and mountainous piles of gravel and sand.

Pulling the letter of acceptance out from her backpack, she double-checked the address. She was in the right place, and the instructions were clear:

"Report to Building 5 at 9:00 a.m. on the first day, and at 7:30 a.m. on subsequent days." The shed before her certainly didn't look like the cheerful, bucolic place she had envisioned, but it was, apparently, where she was supposed to be. The day was not turning out well. With a sigh of disappointment, she locked her bike, removed her helmet and walked down a descending pathway to enter the building.

Inside the lighting was dim and the air smelled of oil and machinery. The shed housed several large lawnmowers and a wide assortment of tools and garden equipment, as well as a small open office area. There were wide doors on one side of the building that could be opened to let out the mowers. No colorful bins of crayons, kazoos, or library paste were evident. Instead, to Ginny's shock, sitting casually on fuel drums and a rough countertop she saw the same group who had yelled at her from the back of the pickup truck, along with their driver. The four appeared to be in their 20s or early 30s. She realized that the truck in the parking space outside was the same pickup that had almost run her over.

Fortunately, without her helmet on they didn't recognize her. Glancing briefly at Ginny, the four returned to their conversation, ignoring her presence.

One of the men had freckles and a messy shock of red hair, which instantly gave him away as the beer-drinking driver. Up close, Dick—for that was his name—had an appearance of innocence. He was short with a wry grin, and if it weren't for his deep voice and thick arms, he could almost have been one of Ginny's elementary-school students, a big brother of Joey Sullivan.

He was staring now at the man from the truck bed who had given Ginny the finger, and said in a blurry voice, "Are you fucking with us, Harry? He smoked that shit? All of it?"

Harry nodded and spit onto the floor. If Ginny had seen him walking down the sidewalk toward her, she would have crossed to the other side of the street. There was something menacing about his slouched, muscular build. Unpleasant-looking tattoos covered his pale arms and ran up his neck. His greasy dark hair was slicked back from his forehead, and he wore the same grim, unsmiling countenance that had sneered at her when she was on her bicycle.

"No shit!" exclaimed Dick. He turned to the other man. "You hear that, Tom?"

"That guy would smoke my dick if he could light a match to it," said Tom. The nicest looking of the three men, he was tall and scrawny, with coffee-colored skin and tightly curled hair.

The young woman, a Latina whose name was Rosie, scooched over and snuggled up closely to Tom, grinding her hip into his side. "And you'd fuckin' love it if he smoked your dick," she said. "I can hear you now. 'Oh, baby, baby, I'm so hot, I'm burnin', I'm burnin', don't stop.'"

"Like hell I would," retorted Tom.

Ginny's face reddened at their conversation. When they paused, she spoke up. "Excuse me? Can anyone here help me?"

One by one, the members of the crew turned away from each other to stare at her rudely. Her question was met with sullen silence. She smiled awkwardly. Nobody smiled back, and her smile faded.

"Excuse me," she repeated, "but is this Building Five?"

After an uncomfortably long beat, Harry curtly said, "Yeah. So?"

"Well, I think maybe someone made a mistake. Maybe there's another Building Five. I was assigned to report to work here. I'm supposed to be teaching arts and recreation?"

Tom mimicked her softly, nodding toward his redheaded comrade and speaking in falsetto: "I think maybe someone made a mistake. Maybe there's another Building Five. Dick was assigned to report to work here."

Ginny gamely attempted another smile, but her solar plexus began to knot in tension. She put her hand on her midsection in a vain attempt to comfort herself. Harry stared silently at her and insolently scratched his groin. Disconcerted, Ginny spotted a phone on the desk in the small office space.

"Do you mind if I use this? Mine's almost out of juice," she asked.

Harry, who appeared to be in charge, shrugged. Ginny crossed to the desk and, looking at the letter, tapped in the number.

"Could you please connect me to Arts and Recreation?" Ginny said into the phone. She was put on hold, and sighed.

Dick continued the high-pitched mimicry that Tom had started: "Could you please connect me to Farts and Copu-lation? That's what I teach."

He leaned to the side and pulled a pint of vodka out from a hiding place behind some tools on a shelf. Twisting off the cap, he took a generous swig.

"Try mastur-bation," said Rosie gleefully. "Don't teach nothin' you don't know, Dicky."

"Hey, hey, smart ass," retorted Dick, wiping his mouth with the back of his hand. "I can fuck anyone, any time!"

"Ain't that your motto, Rosie?" smirked Harry.

"Shut up, Harry," said Rosie. She turned to Dick. "Sure, Dicky. You can fuck anyone any time...so long as they got four legs and go B-a-a-a."

Rosie's thick dark hair was piled high on her head and fastened with clips. She was dressed in pink shorts that were a size too small. Her fleshy midriff bulged out over them, and her ample chest similarly tried its best to spill out from a low-cut halter top. Metal piercings glittered in various places on her face and belly button.

To Ginny's relief, someone finally answered the phone. "Could I please speak to the supervisor?" she said, pausing for replies from the person on the other end of the line. "My name is Ginny Lawson. ... Yes, yes, I'm an employee. Look, here's my situation. I'm supposed to be working for you, starting this morning, at the kid's day camp teaching arts and recrea.... Yes, I did. I got the letter. I have it right here in front of me. They said for me to report to Building Number Five, and that's where I am, but it's like some kind of maintenance shed. I mean, this is definitely not the day camp...."

"What?!" cried out Tom. "This ain't day camp? My mommy's been sendin' me here all these months, and now she tells me?"

Rosie, who was looking out the open door, jumped to her feet. "Be good, boys and girls. Here comes your counselor. Chief Bobby."

"Chief Hard-ass," said Tom, scampering off the counter.

"The day camp is downtown, not here?" said Ginny into the phone. She paused, listening, and then replied, "But I don't understand. How could you not know that?"

"Shit, he wasn't supposed to come until noon," scowled Harry.

As Bob entered the shed, the energy shifted dramatically. The crew suddenly became busy, mutely donning blue coveralls with the park service logo printed across the back. As Dick changed, he snuck a final sip from the vodka bottle and unobtrusively slid it into its hiding place in the back of the shelf.

An unkempt older black man, Bob wore a T-shirt and jeans, and had the weathered skin of someone who has spent most of his life outdoors. His face was rutted with deep creases, his large hands were rough, and he had a full head of graying hair. Even so, there was an air of serious authority about him. It was obvious that he was the boss.

He walked gruffly to the time clock and picked up the time cards, eyeballing them. Then he turned to his desk and for the first time noticed Ginny sitting in his chair, still talking on the phone. He stared sourly down at her.

"Are you absolutely sure? Parks Maintenance?" she was asking. "You don't have anything? ...Yes, all right, I understand. Thank you for...yes, okay. Goodbye."

Crestfallen, Ginny turned the phone off. Then she looked up to see Bob towering above her.

"Oh, is this your desk?" She rose apologetically.

Bob did not reply. Ginny smoothed back her short hair and smiled nervously. "I'm sorry. Was this your phone? I had to use it...but I asked first. They said it was okay."

There was still no response.

"Are you the manager here?" she continued. She glanced at her paper and then back at him. "Are you Bob Corbett?"

"Yeah," he said gruffly.

Ginny smiled harder and extended her hand toward him. He made no move to shake hands with her. She pulled back, flustered.

"Well, you see, I'm supposed to be teaching arts and recreation at the day camp..." she said.

Dick made a loud farting noise. The others laughed at this.

Ginny, flushing, continued, "...and something got messed up. I got assigned to your maintenance crew by mistake. The thing is, it's too late for me to get my job back with the kid's day camp. They mixed up the paperwork, and somebody else got the position, and now they don't have any more openings for what I do."

Tom muttered under his breath lasciviously, "Do me. I got an opening, baby."

Harry looked at Tom and retorted in a whisper that was just loud enough for Ginny to overhear, "You gotta be kiddin'. You would do that old dog?"

Rosie chimed in loudly. "You got two openings, Tommy. They're called holes. One is in your head, and the other one is in your ass."

Bob ignored their comments and spoke tersely to Ginny. "You done with the phone, then?"

It was still in her hand. She put it down on the desk as though she had just been burned. The crude talk and Bob's indifference to her plight were too much for Ginny. All she wanted to do was to leave, and to leave quickly. The space behind the desk was narrow, and she squeezed through clumsily, unable to avoid rubbing up against Bob as the two exchanged places. The crew snickered at this. Ginny felt keenly aware of her breasts and thighs brushing up against him. He stiffened awkwardly, but there was no place for him to escape. To her surprise, he smelled pleasant, a combination of woodsmoke and something else, a natural scent that she couldn't quite put her finger on.

As she made her way toward the exit, Bob picked up a memo from the desk and beckoned for Rosie. The young woman hopped to his side and leaned over his shoulder, peering at the paper. She said something to him in an undertone. Ginny was disappointed by the events of the day, but relieved that at least she was going to be able to get away from these people. She had almost exited when Bob called out after her.

"Are you Virginia Lawson?"

"Virginia?!" echoed Dick in a mocking voice.

Ginny stopped and turned. "Yes, I am. I'm Ginny. Ginny Lawson. How did you know my name?"

Bob tapped the memo. "I asked for extra summer crew. They gave me you."

Ginny gave him a despondent look and sighed. "Look, I am sorry about this. What a mess. I don't have a job any more, and you don't have the help you need. Someone obviously screwed up."

"You can stay."

"What?" she said, her brow furrowing.

"If you want to work, you can stay," said Bob.

"But this is parks maintenance, right? I mean, what is it that you do?"

With a small glimmer of humor, Bob replied, "We maintain the parks."

"Well, I'm a music teacher," said Ginny hesitantly. "I don't have any experience."

Rosie, who had returned to perch on a countertop, kicked up her feet in glee and shouted, "Hey, Harry! She's a cherry!"

Bob glowered at her. "Shut up, Rosie." He turned back to Ginny, and she got another whiff of wood-smoke. He gestured as he spoke. His wide hands were heavily calloused. "You don't need experience."

The crew hooted happily at this.

Ginny shook her head. "Sorry, but I couldn't even if I wanted to. I require a certain basic income."

"Maintenance pays four dollars an hour more, entry level, than any other park position. Including the day camp. Take it or leave it," said Bob disinterestedly.

Dick piped up, saying, "I got a position I'll pay five dollars for. How about it, Rosie?"

Rosie sneered at him and said, "I'll pay ten dollars just to see you try and get it up, booze-for-brains."

Ginny, torn, glanced around the shed reluctantly. Four dollars an hour more than she'd been expecting was tempting. The crew were not tempting. She was accustomed to the familiar, protected world of elementary-school teachers and children. It was a gentle world, and one where she was well liked. But she badly needed more money in the bank.

"Four dollars?" she said. "Gee, I guess I could use the money."

Dick said softly to Rosie, "Gee, I guess I could use the money."

Ginny tried to ignore him and looked at Bob. "If I were to decide to work for you, when would you want me to start?"

Dick patted his zipper, and said to Rosie, "When would you want me to start?"

Rosie lifted her middle finger toward Dick, and then slowly turned her hand around, letting the stiff finger fall limp and droop downward. Bob reached for a shelf behind his desk, grabbed a folded pair of park service coveralls and tossed them to Ginny.

"Now," he said.

CHAPTER FOUR
Cleaning North Park

❦

A SHORT TIME LATER

A SHAFT OF morning light fell on the rustic-looking sign displaying the park's name: North Park. It was one of the four city parks the crew maintained. Each had the uninspired name of one of the four directions. Even though Ginny had driven past the entrance many times, she had never gone through the gates before. North Park turned out to be a traditional city park with picnic tables grouped under a shelter, restrooms, a big playground, old shade trees, a few hiking trails, and a large grassy lawn. A handful of children were already romping in the playground with a small clump of adults standing to the side, watching over them.

Dick, at the wheel of the maintenance truck, drove past the asphalt parking lot, pulled onto a gravel pathway, and squealed to a jerking halt. The cargo bed, it turned out, had jump seats with seat belts. Because Bob was working with them, the crew, including Ginny, had obediently strapped themselves in. After she had agreed to join the maintenance group, he had introduced each of them to her, but they otherwise behaved as if she weren't present. They stood up sluggishly now, yawning and stretching. Hitched to the rear of the truck was a low, wide trailer holding two large riding lawnmowers.

Bob, who had followed in his own pickup truck, pulled up alongside them and bounded out, his truck door slamming noisily behind him. He walked briskly to their vehicle.

"Tom," he called, "get the ramp. Guys, give him a hand. C'mon, snap to it. The day's already half over."

Tom nimbly leapt over the sides of the truck and went to the trailer, where he pulled out a ramp for the tractors. Harry and Rosie jumped down after him and, along with Dick, began unloading the mowers and other work equipment. Ginny had climbed into the back before the trailer had been hitched to the rear of the truck. Now abandoned, she looked around for an easier way out. Seeing none, she hoisted herself awkwardly over the side of the cargo bed, and as she dropped onto the gravel, she stumbled into Bob. He grabbed her elbow to steady her. Their eyes met briefly. Ginny had always felt that a person's soul revealed itself in their eyes. Her own eyes were blue peaceful places where one could come to rest. Bob's darker eyes were carefully shielded, and yet she thought she caught a glimpse of multiple layers hiding underneath the glaze.

"Sorry," she said, ducking her head.

Letting go of her elbow with a start as though surprised that he had been holding onto it, Bob moved rapidly to the rear to help with the mowers. As Ginny stood rooted to the spot, feeling helpless, Rosie came around from the other side of the truck carrying a bucket, mop, and cleaning supplies.

"Move your butt out of the way," said the young woman.

Startled, Ginny took a few steps backward as Rosie brushed past her and began walking up a path that led toward the restrooms.

Tom, who was some yards away, began chanting, "Rosie, Rosie, show us your tit. Rosie, Rosie, show us your tit..."

Rosie transferred the equipment she was carrying to one hand, casually unzipped the top of her coveralls and, without breaking stride, pulled out a bare breast. The crew whooped appreciatively. Ginny watched, stunned. Bob, who was seated in one of the mowers adjusting something, didn't even look up.

Ginny waited to get some instructions. Finally she walked over to Bob and said, "What do you want me to do?"

"Clean the toilets. Follow Rosie," he said, nodding toward the restrooms.

She was about to say something else when he turned on the engine of the mower, drowning her out.

With a sigh, Ginny began to trot after Rosie. "Hey, Rosie, wait up!"

Rosie, who was stuffing her breast back into her top, did not wait up.

AFTER SPENDING THE morning scrubbing the restrooms, the two women finally emerged. Ginny blinked and took in a deep breath.

"Whew! Fresh air! Sunshine! I feel like they just let me out of death row," she said amicably.

Rosie shrugged. "Get used to it," she said as she stacked the equipment she had been carrying in a loose heap on the gravel pathway.

"What time is it, anyway?" Ginny asked, squinting up at the sky.

Not replying, Rosie headed toward the playground. Tom approached from another direction, juggling cans of soda and greasy bags of fast food. Rosie called out loudly to Dick and Harry, who were raking under some trees, "Hey, assholes. Lunch."

Ginny, whose arms were full with a bottle of disinfectant, a mop, and a scrub bucket, took the supplies back to the truck, climbing in clumsily over the trailer hitch. She hauled her knapsack out of a compartment in the back that Bob had unlocked, and then returned to the restroom to wash her hands. When she emerged, she saw that the others had gathered on the playground. The four sat in a cluster on a spinning merry-go-round, displacing the children, who had moved to the far end of the play area. The crew shared their bags of fast food and tossed the drinks back and forth like softballs, laughing with glee when the sodas exploded in huge sprays as they opened them. Ginny trailed up to them and stood for a moment. No one moved to make room for her, so she lowered herself down instead on a nearby bench, pulling out a container of raspberry yogurt and a spoon. Bob was riding the mower in the background, wearing headphones.

Tom said to Harry, "What're you gonna do if he tries it again?"

"Do what I always do. Kick the shit out of him," Harry replied.

Dick, sounding a little drunk, said, "You ever been kicked in the balls?"

"They're always doin' that in the movies, man. WHAM—right in the nuts!" cried Tom. He jumped down off the turntable and demonstrated on Dick, kicking violently in the air and only stopping a few inches short of actual contact. The crew laughed at this.

"Shit, that's what I should do," said Harry. "I should kick him in the fuckin' balls."

Tom came back to his spot and sat down. Rosie half stood and reached over him to grab a handful of French fries, deliberately brushing her breast against his face. Cramming the fries into her mouth, she sat back down and gestured with a grimace at Ginny's lunch.

"What's that?" she said.

"It's yogurt," said Ginny.

"Shut up!" said Rosie. "You mean someone actually eats that crap?"

"Calories," smiled Ginny weakly. "You know."

"Yecch," cried Rosie.

"Oh, it's not so bad," said Ginny. "This kind is sweetened with honey, not sugar. I put berries in it. It's good for you. Some people even think it gives you longevity."

"Longevity?" shouted Tom with a guffaw. "It gives you longevity? Jesus, Dick! Hurry up and eat some of that stuff before she finishes it all!" He turned to the others. "His pecker's so short, takes half an hour for him to find where it is in his pants when he's gotta pee."

Embarrassed, Ginny looked away.

Dick crumpled up an empty food bag and stretched out on his back. "Piss on you," he said.

"Hafta find your dong first before you can piss with it, don'tcha?" sneered Harry.

Tom sat up straighter, grinning. "Me, now I got the opposite problem," he drawled. "I better never touch no yogurt. Mine's so long, girls take one look at it, scream, and run away." He gave Rosie a sidelong glance.

"So that's why you ain't gettin' any," muttered Dick.

"You got it all wrong, Tom-tom," said Rosie tartly. "Girls take one look at your FACE, scream, and run away."

"Hey Tom, I know how you can shorten your dick," said Harry. "Let Rosie touch it. Guaranteed—shrivel any guy's cock in two seconds flat."

"Up yours," said Rosie.

Tom turned to look at Dick. "Is that what happened to your cock then? Rosie touched it?"

Dick belched in response. In the background Bob stopped the mower on the grass next to his truck. Opening the door, he removed a brown lunch bag from the front seat and walked over to the picnic shelter. Ginny watched him curiously for a moment, and then turned to the crew, making an effort to be social.

"Do you all like working here—for the parks?" she asked.

In response, the crew simply snickered. Rosie rolled her eyes sarcastically and got off the turntable. Moving to a swing, she began to pump herself higher and higher.

Ginny pretended to ignore the rebuff. She persisted. "Do most of you live around here? In the area? Actually, myself, I only live less than two miles..."

Interrupting her impatiently, Rosie shouted, "We all commute from our fuckin' mansions on the Mediterranean, okay?"

Ginny bit her lip. She was grateful that there were no children in their immediate vicinity. Just then a squirrel ran past, and Harry took aim with an imaginary rifle. He pulled the trigger, making explosive sound effects.

"Wish I had my .22," he said. "Shoot the ass clean off that fucker."

"Oh, yeah, like when we went deer-huntin' last Thanksgiving. Remember that?" said Tom.

"Shut up," said Harry.

"What?" cried Rosie from the swings, her interest perked. "What'd you do, Harry?" She turned to the others. "What'd he do?"

Tom brayed loudly, the pitch of his voice rising, "He shot a deer right in the ass! I'm not kiddin'! Shot its tail right off. Deer goes runnin' into the woods with its ass all bloody, and there's this white tail lyin' on the ground. Harry mounted it. It's hangin' over his bed."

"Hey, congratulations!" said Rosie. "Finally got some tail into your bedroom, Harry."

They all laughed except Ginny, who had turned away with a shiver at the cruel story. Her eyes caught those of a little boy, about four years old, who was wandering alone at the edge of the playground in tears. Ginny immediately jumped up from her bench and ran over to help.

Catching up with the boy, she knelt down and held him gently by the arms, breathing in his scent. "Oh, honey, what's the matter?"

The little boy kept on crying.

"Did you lose someone?"

"My mommy!" The boy's lower lip quivered and he burst into fresh sobs.

Ginny gave him a tender hug. Then she rose, taking his hand. "Let's look for her. I know she's here. Where can she be?" Pointing to a small cluster of women and children who had gathered near the slides, she said, "Is that mommy over there?"

The little boy broke free and ran wildly toward the group. "MOMMY!" he called, as a young pregnant woman responded, rushing toward him with open arms.

Ginny smiled. Then, turning back to the crew who had begun spinning boisterously on the carousel, her smile faded and she sighed. Bob, eating his lunch at a distance, watched closely.

CHAPTER FIVE
Pizza with Tracy

⨯

THAT NIGHT

G INNY LIVED ON the first floor of a brownstone that was old enough both to be quaint and to require constant repairs. There were aging decorative plaster moldings on the high ceilings, and the restored woodwork around the door frames and baseboards was elaborate, but the floors were treacherously slanted, and she was constantly battling cockroaches. Her small living room spilled over with plants, Impressionist prints of gardens and flowers, books, and colorful knickknacks. Piles of music lay on top of a piano, and the coffee table displayed several days' worth of junk mail from assorted charities.

Sharing the flat with Ginny was Muffin, a large, reddish-colored, long-haired dog of indeterminate breed. She was trying unsuccessfully to shoo him off the couch when the doorbell rang. It was Tracy, carrying a white pizza box. Muffin clamored down from the sofa and began to twirl around the blonde visitor in a welcoming frenzy.

"Relief for the working woman," shouted Tracy cheerfully, holding the pizza higher than the dog could reach.

Ginny, who had changed into baggy sweatpants and a T-shirt, was too exhausted to smile. "Down, Muffin," she commanded in a tired voice. The dog only half obeyed. Ginny bent over to scratch him behind his ears. "You need to go out?" She gestured toward the open door.

The dog ignored the opportunity and instead jammed his body up against Tracy, his bushy tail wagging furiously.

"I think Muffin believes that he needs some pizza," said Tracy. "I know I do."

Ginny closed the door behind them. "Sorry about the mess," she said, trying to clear a space for the pizza on the coffee table and glancing around in dismay at the clutter. As she went into the kitchen to get drinks, she called out, "I don't know what's happening to me. I used to be so organized. I think this place is getting too small. Time for a change. ...You got vegetarian?" She re-entered with two bottles of soda.

"I went to Pancho's Pizzeria," said Tracy. "Pancho swore to me that the only living things that were killed to make this pizza were tomatoes, peppers, and mushrooms," she announced. "And broccoli."

"Goody. I'm ravenous. All I had for lunch was a little thingy of yogurt."

"What's the soda?" asked Tracy.

"Ginger ale," replied Ginny. "Organic."

"Of course. God, I am getting so healthy hanging out with you!"

The women lowered themselves onto the floor next to the coffee table and began to attack the pizza. A few greasy peppers slid off Tracy's slice onto the wooden floor.

"Whoopsie! Sorry," she said.

"All yours, Muffin," sighed Ginny.

Muffin ran to the spot, his toenails scrabbling against the floor, and eagerly lapped up the spill.

"The grease will be good for the wood," mumbled Tracy apologetically.

Ginny didn't seem to care. "I suppose we should really sit in the dining room," she said, "but I'm too worn out to move."

Tracy looked at her shrewdly as she blew on her pizza slice to cool it off. "So these new little co-workers of yours...super obnoxious, huh?"

Ginny closed her eyes and rubbed her temples, trying to dispel some of the tension that had collected there.

"Obnoxious doesn't even come close," she said. "Tracy, they are completely disgusting. I'm used to kids misbehaving. I'm patient. You know I am. But they were over the top. I tried so hard to be polite—I really did. Nothing works with them. They're just plain nasty. When I came home after work, I fell down on the couch and cried for fifteen minutes."

"That only means they win, you know," said Tracy, pulling a long strand of melted cheese off her slice of pizza and dangling it into her mouth.

"Yeah, well I never signed up for a battle. Going to work shouldn't about winning or being conquered."

"So? Dish it right back," said Tracy.

"I refuse to stoop to their level! I wouldn't even know how to get on their level. Every word out of their mouths is obscene. And juvenile." Ginny toyed listlessly with her plate.

"Then do what we do at school: send 'em to the principal's office!"

"The principal?" Ginny finally lifted a slice of pizza up to her mouth and bit into the end, chewing and swallowing it before she spoke. A piece of mushroom stuck on the side of her mouth unnoticed. "That would be Bob. Bob is the boss. He doesn't care. He's another one of them, only older and bossier. Do you know what he made me do all day? I scrubbed toilets. Filthy toilets. City park toilets."

"The scoundrel! He sounds so mean," retorted Tracy with a laugh, reaching over to brush the mushroom piece off Ginny's face.

"He has nice eyes, though," Ginny mused, almost as if she were talking to herself. "There's something about him…." She shook herself back. "It's probably my imagination. They are all awful, all of them."

"Are you going to go back tomorrow, then?

Ginny groaned. She reached for her bottle of ginger ale and took a swig before answering. "I guess so," she said. "It's money. I need the money. It would take me all summer just to find another job."

Tracy tore a small greenish piece from her pizza slice and held it out toward the dog, who had been staring alternately at her mouth and at her plate with great intensity as she ate. It was obvious that he had a history of receiving table treats from Tracy.

"Okay, Muffin. Try some broccoli."

Lunging to her side, the dog chomped eagerly at the bit of food on her outstretched hand.

"Your dog likes broccoli! When did they start putting broccoli on pizza, anyway?" said Tracy.

Ginny didn't hear her. She was still thinking about Bob's eyes, wondering what was beneath all the layers.

CHAPTER SIX
Restrooms and Raspberries

TUESDAY

G INNY ARRIVED AT the shed early and waited outside, scuffing her shoes restlessly in the dirt until Harry showed up with a key and silently unlocked the door. Tom and Rosie appeared shortly afterward, and they immediately went over to the time cards hanging in metal slots on the wall near Bob's desk. The names of each of the crew members had been awkwardly printed in big letters above their individual time cards. VIRGINIA had now been added to the names, with a clean time card beneath.

"Can someone show me how this works?" asked Ginny.

Elbowing Tom and Rosie out of the way, Harry gestured for Ginny to come closer, and gruffly showed her how to punch her card into the electric time clock. Ginny did not like being close to Harry. He smelled unpleasantly of sweat and stale cigarette smoke. After she had finished, the others followed suit. When Tom's turn came, he waggled his tongue suggestively at Rosie.

A few moments later, as the four were pulling on their coveralls, Dick stumbled in and headed for the time clock. "Shit, I've got a headache."

He looked awful, with dark circles under his eyes. After punching in, he sank to the floor and covered his head miserably with his hands, making little groaning sounds.

Rosie, who had finished dressing, heaved herself up onto a heavy work table and taunted him while she put clips into her hair: "Is Dicky-boy hung over?"

"Yeah. I'm hung," moaned Dick.

"Like hell you are," said Tom.

Ginny had hoped that their juvenile banter of the previous day had been a fleeting phenomenon. She was mistaken.

"C'mon, gimme a fucking break. I'm in misery here," Dick said, his head still in his hands.

"A fucking break? You mean you want a break for fucking?" asked Tom gaily, clapping him on the shoulder. "Best idea you've ever come up with, Dicky!"

There was a shelf near the time clock where they kept their belongings. Ginny extracted her backpack from its designated cubbyhole, unzipped one of the compartments, and pulled out a bottle of white pills.

"Drugs?" Rosie exclaimed gleefully. "You carry drugs in that thing?"

"All *right!*" said Tom, stiffening in military fashion and giving Ginny a salute.

Ignoring them, Ginny proffered the bottle to Dick. "Would you like some aspirin?"

"Oh Jesus, yes," he said miserably.

As he reached for the bottle, Harry swiped it and, with a snort, tossed it to Tom. The two pitched it back and forth over Dick's head. He grabbed for the pills in vain.

"You cock-suckin' apes, gimme my aspirins. MY ASPIRINS!"

"Hey dude, if your ass burns, shove it in a bucket of ice water," crowed Rosie joyously.

There was a gleam of light from the open door as Bob suddenly entered the shed. Harry quickly dropped the aspirin bottle, and Dick crawled after it on his hands and knees.

Bob was clenching an instruction booklet in his hand. He did not look happy. On the cover of the pamphlet was a scene of pastoral green fields and colorful flowers. He beckoned to Rosie. "Come here." He opened the booklet and pointed to a section, holding it out for her to read. "Tell me what it says right there."

"Caution," she read, stumbling over some of the words, her voice wooden. "Keep children, birds and animals away from sprayed area for at least 24 hours. Do not ingest, inhale, or expose to skin, eyes, or mucous membranes. If exposure occurs, immediately flush with..."

"That's enough," he said, grim-lipped.

Snatching the pamphlet back, he picked up the phone on his desk to make a call. Ginny watched him curiously. After entering the number, Bob raised his eyes to meet hers, staring back at her as if in challenge. She quickly looked away and turned to Dick to retrieve her aspirin bottle.

While Bob waited for the other end to answer, Tom and Harry began to spar with garden trowels. They reminded Ginny of some of the nine-year-old boys in her music class.

Turning his back on the crew, Bob began speaking, tapping his index finger impatiently on the desk as he talked. "Corbett here.... Yeah, yeah, it came. Delivered this morning. But listen. It's gotta go back. I'm not using that stuff.... Because it's *poison*, that's why. I'm not going to go around spraying poison on.... No, they won't. Not if you send it back, they.... So take the goddamn shipping charges out of my paycheck!"

He ended the call angrily and glared at the crew as he slammed the phone down on the desk. Used to taking the pulse of his moods, Tom and Harry immediately stopped horsing around and tossed the trowels into bins of equipment, each picking up a crate. As they filed out the door, Dick and Ginny were the first to step into the daylight. The sun made Dick's hair look even redder.

"Thanks," he mumbled to her, smiling weakly.

"You're welcome," she replied. "Any time at all. Just ask."

Dick nodded his head. Their small moment of courtesy was shattered instantly by a snicker from Rosie, and then by Tom's voice as he emerged from the hut: "Did you see that part in *The Shout* where he rips the guy's face off and starts eatin' it?"

Tom stopped momentarily in the doorway, looking back for approval at Harry, who was following closely on his heels.

"Man, that was so dope," nodded Harry. "And then his brains start oozin' outta his eyeballs!"

Tom loaded the crate that he was carrying onto the trailer and then lunged toward Dick, pushing him against the side of the truck. He pretended to rip his face off and eat it, making slurping sounds. Dick shoved him away in annoyance. Tom stumbled into Rosie, where he pantomimed the same thing.

"Hey, hey, you prick," cried Rosie. "Don't eat me!"

"Now there's a first," muttered Harry.

Bob, ignoring their antics, pointed brusquely at several flats of flowers sitting on the back of his pickup truck. "Load these onto the trailer. Snap to it. We're planting them today."

Ginny brightened visibly. The flowers, dozens of multi-colored pansies, petunias, and orange marigolds, looked healthy and cheerful. "Goody," she said.

Tom noticed her reaction. Mimicking her and speaking in a cartoon voice, he cried out, "Ooh, goody-gumdrops! We're going to plant lovely little flowers today! Tra-lah!"

He pranced around the flowers, singing and skipping, while Dick and Harry complied with Bob's order, beginning to heave the flats onto the trailer.

Bob, who was putting tools onto the seat of his truck, turned toward them angrily. "Tom, get to work. And I didn't say *throw* 'em. I said *load* 'em!"

Rosie lifted up a flat of red petunias and walked toward the men. Speaking in a softer voice, out of Bob's earshot, she said, "Boy, does the boss ever need to get laid!"

"You volunteering, Rosie?" said Harry, who had climbed into the trailer. He took the flowers from her and put them down with exaggerated caution.

"I'll bet you a hundred bucks that he hasn't balled anyone for seven years, not since his old lady died," Rosie said, tossing her head in Bob's direction.

"I believe that," muttered Tom, handing Harry another flat.

Bob walked back to the shed, still holding the booklet, which he was crumpling in his fist. His knuckles and jaw were clenched. He was obviously irritated. "Step on it, you guys," he called angrily over his shoulder before he went inside. "I've got another load waiting for me to pick up."

Ginny stood helplessly next to the flowers. The rest of the crew were lifting and loading the pallets. They had fallen into a work rhythm that did not include her.

"He's a widower?" she asked.

Rosie gave her a brief, rude glance.

"Bob? He's a widower?" Ginny persisted. "His wife is dead?" If his wife had died, she thought, it would explain a lot about a certain vibration—a low level of a kind of sad isolation—that emanated from him.

Rosie, picking up another flat of petunias, still didn't respond. Ginny felt as though she had been punched in the stomach. Noticing her helplessness, after a beat of silence Dick spoke up.

"Yeah. His wife died. Long time ago."

THEY DROVE TO West Park, which had large garden beds. Despite their childishness and crudity, all the members of the crew were capable of working hard and fast when pushed to do so. Even Rosie was surprisingly strong. As soon as they arrived, before Ginny could even unfasten the belt from her jump seat on the back of the truck, Harry and Tom had leaped over the side and begun to unload the flats of flowers from the trailer. Dick climbed out of the driver's seat and joined them.

"Did you guys see *The Shout II?*" he asked, grunting as he hoisted up a box of bright orange marigolds.

Tom grabbed a flat. "Best part was when he hacked off the guy's foot with the saw and there's blood spurtin' all the way across the room."

"No shit, man!" said Dick, starting down the path. "That was awesome!"

Harry, the fastest of them, was already returning down the path from the groomed beds for a second flat of flowers. "Nu-uh," he said. "Best fuckin' part? Right before the end, when they exploded that bitch..." He paused to make the sound of an explosion: "...an' a piece of her skin flies right across the windshield! Spl-a-a-a-t!"

As Harry picked up the next box of flowers, Tom and Dick assented enthusiastically from the path, hooting out noisy sound effects.

Deciding that it was time to join them, Ginny lifted a smaller box of pansies that rested near the edge of the trailer, and headed down the path, trailing after the men. The flowers were a little bit heavy, but she didn't mind. She liked gardening and was even mildly excited at the idea of planting. It might turn out to be a nice day after all, if she could ignore the crudities of the crew.

Just then Bob pulled up in his truck, which was filled with more pallets of blossoms. He called out after her, "What are you doing?"

Ginny paused, turned, and answered him with a tinge of sarcasm. "I'm planting flowers?"

"No, you're not," scowled Bob. "You go with Rosie. I need you girls to clean out the toilets."

Ginny's smile fell. Rosie, carrying buckets and a mop, had already started trudging toward the restrooms.

THE RESTROOM SMELLED vile. Ginny, grateful to find a face mask and rubber gloves among the supplies, put them on, hesitantly knelt next to a toilet, and began scrubbing. There were six stalls. It was painstaking, nasty work. Rosie, scouring the fixtures without a mask, finished hers first and moved to the next toilet stall. Looking in, she made a face.

"Eeeew," she cried. "Who did this?! What kinda asshole comes to a city park to take a crap? Why don't they shit at home! Don't they know we gotta smell this stuff? Don't they know how to flush?"

"Maybe it was a little kid," said Ginny. She did not like cleaning toilets. As a teacher of young children, however, she had learned to deal with frequent accidents of all kinds and had taught herself to push through the unpleasantness that accompanies being a human being without letting it get to her.

"Little kid, my ass. No little kid could shit this big!"

Ginny rose, her knees stiff, to move to the next stall, and stubbed her toe on the doorframe. "Oh darn it!" she exclaimed.

Rosie sat back on her heels and cocked her head around the corner to mock Ginny. "'Darn it? DARN it?!' Someone in the world actually says that: '*darn it*?' Sheesh. Why don't you say 'Goddamn fucking son-of-a-bitch' when you hurt yourself, like everybody else does?"

Answering her patiently, Ginny said, "Rosie, not 'everybody else' does. Not everyone on the planet finds it necessary to use ugly language."

"Depends on which planet you come from. Mine happens to be called Earth. What's yours called?"

"I don't like to swear," said Ginny, tightening her lips.

"How come? Are you, like, some kinda religious nut?" asked Rosie.

"No," said Ginny sharply. Catching herself, she spoke more calmly and deliberately, the way she would address one of her young students. "Using bad language makes other people feel uncomfortable, Rosie."

Rosie snorted.

"Besides," added Ginny, "I was always taught— and I believe—that swearing is the sign of someone who has a limited vocabulary."

"Huh?" said the other woman.

"Someone of lower intelligence," sighed Ginny.

Rosie shifted her attention back inside her stall and stared at the toilet. "Would you look at the size of this mother-fuckin' shit!"

A FEW HOURS later when the crew were seated around one of the picnic tables in the park, taking their lunch break, Bob pulled up in his truck, carrying another load of flower pallets. Ginny felt a curious sense of relief at seeing him. Even though yesterday he had left them alone at mealtime, today he removed a wooden pint box from his passenger seat and began to walk toward the group.

"Oh, great. Here comes Blob," muttered Rosie.

Dick turned to Ginny. "So you're a teacher, right?"

"Yes," she replied guardedly.

He reflected on this for a moment. "What do you teach?"

Ginny perked up a little at hearing a friendly question. Bob had come within earshot, and in a strange way, she wanted him to overhear her answer.

"Music," she said. "I teach music. To little kids in grade school."

"No shit!" said Dick.

Bob gruffly set the box that he was carrying down on the picnic table in front of the crew. "Raspberries here. If anybody wants 'em," he said.

Ginny scooted over to see. The berries were deep red, ripe, and larger than those one would find in a grocery store. "Oh, they're gorgeous," she said, looking up at him. "Did you grow these?"

Bob nodded in assent.

Rosie, who seemed always happy to disturb a pleasant scene, said with unnecessary vehemence, "Ugh. I *hate* raspberries."

Harry took the opportunity to make a raspberry noise. "Fuckin' little seeds always get stuck in your teeth," he said.

"Yeah," agreed Tom, following Harry's lead. "Too hard to eat."

Ginny took a few of the deep red berries in her hand. There was a curious velvety softness to them. "That's only because you don't know how to eat them," she said. "There's a secret to eating raspberries. What you do is this: you have to put them gently in your mouth...." She demonstrated. "Then you sort of gum them with your tongue until you're ready to swallow. See, the secret is that you don't bite down on them. You never use your teeth."

The crew burst out in leering guffaws. Ginny, taken by surprise, looked at Bob in a silent appeal for help. Abandoning her, he turned and strode back to his truck.

Tom said, "Oh God, I'm gettin' a hard-on!" He seized Rosie's arm and pushed her onto her knees in front of him. She played along. "Oh, oh, do me now, baby, exactly like she said! Before I cream in my overalls."

"Me next," called out Dick happily.

Harry glanced at Ginny, and then said to Rosie, "You heard the teacher, Rosie. Gum it with your tongue till you're ready to swallow, and never use your teeth."

It had taken two days to reach this point, but Ginny was angry.

"You really disgust me, all of you!" she cried, jumping up from her seat. "This is just fruit, for gosh sakes. It's not pornography!"

Rosie suddenly stood, shoving Tom away forcefully. "Hey! I don't do no fruits! Do each other!"

The crew laughed uproariously.

CHAPTER SEVEN
Ginny Finally Gets a Thumbs-Up

❧

THE NEXT DAYS

OVER AND OVER the scene repeated itself: Bob, in dappled sunlight under the towering trees, would ride on the big mower, wearing headphones, while Ginny spent hour after hour on her knees in dark, dank, graffiti-and-garbage-strewn restrooms, scrubbing stained toilet bowls and rusty sinks with Rosie. Rosie would always make crude comments about the filth, while taking every opportunity to crowd her way into Ginny's space, barely stopping short of actually shoving her. When they were outside, one of the men would inevitably chant, "Rosie, Rosie, show us your tit," and unless she was in a bad mood, her breasts would be flashed without comment.

Just like the little boys in Ginny's classrooms, Tom and Harry frequently grabbed sticks, screwdrivers, parking cones, or anything else even moderately phallic to engage in vigorous pretend fights. More than once when Bob wasn't around, they would take up rakes and hold them high in the air like medieval jousters as they approached one another on lawn mowers.

A WEEK PASSED, and Ginny shared the dreary details of work with a visiting Tracy, who looked at her friend in astonishment.

"You had to clean the bathrooms *again?*" she said, her eyes widening.

"It's almost like a game," complained Ginny. "Sometimes the guys rake. Other times, they have nets to clean out the fountains, or they plant, or they trim, or they dig. It doesn't matter what they're doing. They get out of the truck, I follow them, Bob shakes his head no, and points to the toilets. This has happened every single day, Tracy. *Every single day*. It is so rampantly sexist! And those people are unbelievably gross. When I'm not scrubbing toilets, I'm listening to toilet talk. It's gotten so that I dread going to work."

"Why keep on doing it, then? Quit!"

"Tracy, we've been over this," she replied. Her tone of voice had a defensive edge to it. "Where else can I earn money? The college kids have snapped up all the summer jobs."

"Who cares," said the blonde woman. "You're a music teacher. You can think of something. Teach piano. Give singing lessons. Run your own day camp."

"Don't think I haven't thought about that. But it takes time to hustle up private students. It isn't as easy as it sounds," said Ginny. "You know how I got slammed last spring: my teeth needed crowns, the transmission fell out of my car, my couch literally broke underneath me...it was one thing after the other." She sighed deeply. "And the park job pays pretty well. No benefits, of course, but you know what? It actually pays better than what we get teaching."

"That doesn't matter if they're driving you crazy," said Tracy with a shrug.

"Yeah, well I keep thinking to myself that it's only a few months more, and then it's over," said Ginny. "If I can hold on. And by then I'll have some money in the bank again."

FRIDAY CAME, AND Dick was getting ready as usual to climb into the front seat of the truck hauling the lawn mowers. Bob stopped him and sent him to the back to join the others, climbing into the driver's seat himself. The crew clambered into the open cargo bay and, because Bob was with them, dutifully strapped themselves into their jump seats. Someone had brought along a portable speaker, and as they pulled away from the shed the music began booming loudly.

Dick, already slightly inebriated, was sneaking drinks as usual from a bottle of vodka. Ginny sat on his far side, next to the cab. She was sensitive to sound and she hated the music the others listened to. The strident noise and harsh words spilling out of the speaker struck at her nerves like jabs from a sharp needle, and the rumble of the bass through the metal of the cargo bay made her feel as though she were leaning against a concrete mixer. She drew up her knees and pulled herself as far away from the speaker as possible. The crew had to shout to be heard above the vibrating beats.

"Yup, you can lay seven silver dollars on it end to end when it's stiff," Dick was proclaiming.

Harry snickered loudly, "When is it ever stiff?"

Rosie shouted, "Yeah, Dicky. There's a difference between *being* stiff—which you are—and *gettin'* stiff—which you ain't been in years."

Harry chimed in: "And being *a* stiff. Like what's gonna happen soon to the Blob's old lady." He leaned back with a rare smile, pleased with himself.

"You really think he'll take time off when she croaks?" Tom shouted.

"He'll take time off," replied Harry with assurance.

"Then it's party, party, party!" cried Dick.

Ginny had been trying to be a good sport about the music, but she couldn't endure any more. Sticking her neck out so that the others could see her, she gestured toward the speaker and said loudly, "Would someone turn that down, please?"

Nobody moved.

"Hey, would you turn it down?" she repeated, shouting this time.

There was still no response. She couldn't believe that Bob would let them blast the streets with noise, destroying the morning's peace for everyone within earshot. Her indignation rose almost palpably. "C'mon. It's too loud. Please!"

Dick finally pulled out his cellphone. Apparently the music was in his control. To her relief, he lowered the volume.

"Goddamn teacher thinks we're in school," Harry said, his head turned away from her, but loudly enough so that she could hear.

Dick turned to her. "So," he asked, "whaddya want to listen to? Brahms? Bach? Beethoven? What?"

Ginny thought for a moment and then, calling his bluff, said, "Bach."

The red-head fussed with his phone for a moment, and some quiet Baroque music began to play. Dick bowed toward her with an eloquently sweeping gesture, and then settled back, phone in hand.

"Thank you," she said with relief, as the others groaned.

Rosie, Tom, and Harry soon became engaged in hooting and making lewd comments about some naked mannequins they saw in a storefront window that they were driving past. Dick took the opportunity to converse with Ginny.

"So...do you like teaching music?"

"Yes, as a matter of fact I do, Dick. I really love it," she replied.

"Whaddya play?" he asked. "Like, do you play the violin, or the harp, or what?"

"The harp? What makes you say that?" laughed Ginny.

He shrugged and took another drink.

"I play the piano a little," she said. "Mostly I sing."

Dick then gestured at the speaker with his phone and wrinkled his freckled nose. "You're really into this classical shit, huh?"

Harry, bringing his attention back inside the truck, gave Ginny a sullen glance, and apparently decided that he'd had enough of the classical music. "Oh for Christ's sake," he muttered sourly as he grabbed the phone from Dick's hand, changing the music back to its original station. He did not, however, turn the volume back up.

Swiveling around from looking out at the street, Rosie said, "Bob's old lady just better fuckin' not die for another seven weeks, that's all I gotta say." The cab window was closed, so Bob couldn't hear her.

"How come?" asked Harry.

"Because that's the date I chose for the pool, Harry-the-fairy, and I intend to win," she said.

Tom said dejectedly, "I already lost. My day was June 5th."

Rosie pointed to each member of the crew, including herself, as she counted aloud: "Twenty, forty, sixty, eighty fuckin' bucks. All mine in seven weeks! Even if I have to go to Pine Haven and smother her little gray head under a pillow."

"But are you allowed to win the pool if you murder her?" Dick asked.

"I bet September 21," said Harry. "She croaks on September 21."

Confused, Ginny said, "Are you talking about Bob? Didn't Bob's wife already die?" She glanced at the back of his head through the window of the cab.

"Yeah," answered Tom. "So?"

"But I don't understand. You're saying his 'old lady' is getting ready to die?"

"His *mother*," explained Dick. "The boss's mother is the one who's dying. In Pine Haven Rest Home. The mother of the Blob." Dick took another generous swallow of vodka, and, shifting away from Ginny, turned toward the others, gesturing toward his crotch. "Seven silver dollars. Laid end to end."

"Shit, man, that's nothin'," said Tom. "Mine's so long, if I was sitting in a tree with my fly open and Rosie walked underneath, it would whack her in the face."

Harry leered at Rosie: "So next time you walk under a tree, Rosie, do it with your mouth wide open...just in case."

Rosie stared at Harry, held her hand up, and rubbed her thumb and forefinger back and forth. Harry sneered at her and, imitating the gesture, said, "What's this?"

They were pulling into the entrance to South Park. Unbuckling her seat belt, Rosie said, "Me givin' you a hand job." She did a little shimmy with her shoulders.

Tom and Dick howled with laughter.

"Goddamn bitch," said Harry. "You don't know nothin'."

The truck came to a stop. Hastened by Bob's presence, Harry, Tom, and Dick immediately jumped out of the cargo bed and began to unload the lawnmowers, while Rosie gathered up the restroom cleaning equipment. Bob came around the side of the truck and bumped into Ginny as she stumbled down over the side of the cargo bay, colliding with her yet again. After steadying her by her arms, he moved back, giving her a wide berth.

"Harry, Tom—get on the mowers," he commanded briskly. "Dick, you come with me to the tennis courts. You two," he said, gesturing toward Ginny and Rosie, "clean the toilets."

Ginny was ready to obey when a wave of angry defiance swept over her. She stopped rebelliously and stood with her feet planted wide apart on the asphalt of the parking lot, glaring at Bob and the crew as they busied themselves for the work day ahead. The sensations that were beginning to erupt surprised her, for despite her brief outburst on the second day of work, she was usually an even-tempered woman who rarely lost her equanimity. Maybe it was the effect of the loud music on her nerves, or maybe it was simply that the frustration that had been building up over the past days had grown too large to contain. The dam holding her feelings in check blew apart, and a flood of fury rushed out, overtaking her in a matter of seconds. She could scarcely see straight. It came to her with surprise that she was going to yell, and with even more surprise, she realized that it didn't matter to her whether she got fired or whether she ever saw those people again.

"You know what?" she shouted furiously. "I am getting very, very tired of listening to all of your vulgarity!" Hearing the rage in her voice, the crew froze and stared back at her in shock. "Can't you think of anything else to talk about but the size of your genitalia?!"

She turned to Bob with clenched fists, her voice rising. "And I'm REALLY getting tired of cleaning bathrooms! What's the matter with you, anyhow? Just because I have a...a VAGINA, you think that gives me some kind of magic ability to clean a toilet bowl better than a person with a penis?! Well, you're WRONG! Fire me if you want, but I am NOT going to clean toilets today!"

With that, the crew broke free from their momentary paralysis. They snorted and hollered wildly at her words, jabbing one another in glee. Bob was taken aback. Ginny stood her ground, glowering at him in confrontation.

After a pause, he shifted his shoulders, lifted his eyebrows, gave her a brief nod, and said, "Okay. You and Rosie, take the mowers. Harry? Tom?" Bob gestured with his chin toward the restrooms.

Harry scowled angrily and spit. Tom groaned as Rosie triumphantly skipped over to him and handed him the cleaning equipment. "Shit," he said.

Flaunting and waggling her hips, Rosie crowed, "I have a VAGINA!"

She turned to Ginny, giving her a broad smile and a thumbs-up sign. Ginny grinned back, and then, with a deep breath, climbed onto a mower.

CHAPTER EIGHT
The Invitation

STILL FRIDAY

BY THE DAY'S end, Ginny had mastered the mower. Even though she'd worn the earplugs Bob had handed her, the machine had been loud, and she felt frazzled. She understood now why he always wore heavy headphones rather than earbuds when he mowed. Still, enduring the noise and fumes was, in her mind, an acceptable trade-off for the wretchedness of cleaning toilets all day.

As she approached the ramp behind the pickup truck with the mower, Bob came over and began to guide her into position.

"I confess that I have absolutely no experience driving lawn mowers up onto trailers," she said to him with an apologetic smile.

He gave her a rare smile back, and as he directed her, the two moved into a nice rhythm, both effortlessly understanding what the other was indicating. It surprised her.

When the mower was in the right spot, she climbed off the seat, still vibrating a little from so many hours on the machine, and pulled out her earplugs. Bob, who by then was standing next to her on the trailer, leaned in closely as he showed her how to anchor the mower. Their hands brushed for an instant. She felt a heightened awareness of that contact, and sensed that he did as well.

"Thanks for the earplugs," she said.

Bob shrugged and turned his back to her, saying nothing as he climbed down and walked away. Sometimes it seemed as if he were choosing deliberately to destroy any tiny bit of camaraderie that got a chance to build between them.

Ginny climbed down off the trailer. Dick, who was by this time intoxicated, staggered toward her. He tried to grab her around the waist as she hopped to the ground.

"Hey, teach, you were pretty damn cool this morning. I'm wondering. Would'cha like to have a drink...?"

Ginny jerked herself out of his grasp, grimacing at his alcohol-laden breath, and held him off with a stiffened arm. She shook her head, imagining that he was ready to pull out his flask and offer it to her.

"...'Cause it's Friday," he continued, oblivious to her rejection, "and we guys always go out together after work for drinks on Friday. It's a tradition!" He turned to the rest of the crew, who were by now within earshot. "Right?"

Tom grunted something unintelligible, and Rosie rolled her eyes.

Dick turned back to Ginny and, with the concentrated effort of someone nearly too inebriated to speak, said, "So I'm inviting you to come along and share in our tradition. Get to know your co-workers! Have a drink with us! On me! Who knows? Maybe you'll like us!"

He looked at the crew, reaching out with his hands palms-up and gesturing with his fingers for them to support him.

"Yeah, come along," growled Harry. Under his breath he muttered, "Fuckin' day couldn't get no worse anyhow."

"What the hell," sighed Rosie half-heartedly.

Ginny thought about it for a moment. It was obvious that, apart from Dick, the crew didn't want her to come. She wasn't excited about going out with them either, but she realized that if she turned down the invitation to socialize, they would continue to foster the image they had of her as an uptight school teacher for the rest of the summer. After her surprise outburst in the morning, the four had backed off conspicuously from their nasty remarks. She decided to take advantage of this momentary lull in their behavior. It just might be that they would act friendlier if she went along with them.

"Well...all right. I'll come," she said. "Only for a little while, though."

Dick smiled, danced an unsteady little jig, and called exuberantly to Bob, who was busy picking up some equipment several yards away. "You come too, boss! Come to Lefty's. Hell, it's Friday. Unwind! Relax! Have a few laughs with us! Come!"

"If the teacher and the boss come together, is that a simultaneous orgasm?" muttered Tom with a snicker.

"No, it's Dick in the shithouse," whispered Rosie. "Dick, are you fuckin' crazy? We don't want Bob along! Stop kissin' ass!

"Don't worry," said Harry. "The boss ain't gonna come. He always goes to Pine Haven after work to see his mother."

"You know who his mother is, Rosie," smirked Tom. "That's the one you're planning to kill so's you can win the bet."

"He'll say no," insisted Harry.

"Yeah, he'll say no. The Blob'll say no," said Tom.

Dick hollered more loudly. "You comin' or not, boss?"

Walking to the truck and opening the door to the cab, Bob glanced quickly at Ginny. "Okay," he said.

CHAPTER NINE
Lefty's

THAT NIGHT

LEFTY'S WAS A noisy, dimly lit bar that smelled like stale spilled beer. The booths and the seats of the chairs at the scattered tables were upholstered in cheap red vinyl. More than a few of the cushions looked as though they had been deliberately slashed, with ungainly yellowing foam spilling out from the cuts in the plastic as if gasping for air. Peeling brown linoleum covered the floor. Someone had attempted to beautify the room by stringing numerous strands of small multi-colored Christmas lights back and forth across the ceiling; the effect was more garish than pretty, but it drew the eye away from the uglier corners of the establishment.

Ginny stood at the bar, with its requisite mirrored shelves of glasses and bottles behind the bartender, and decided to order a cup of coffee. As the bartender went over to the coffee maker to fill her mug, she watched the crew in the mirror. They had arrived a few minutes before her and had gotten a large pitcher of beer. Juggling empty glasses and the pitcher, Harry, Tom, and Rosie were sliding into a booth that seated four, making their usual noisy wisecracks. Dick plopped down next to them, carefully arranging three shot glasses of vodka in front of him. This was apparently his customary order. Everyone except Rosie wore the same T-shirts they'd had on at work that day under their coveralls. She, however, had changed into a low-cut chartreuse tank top, and she had inserted multi-colored glittering rhinestones into the piercings lining her ears and eyebrows, as well as one under the side of her mouth where she usually hosted a metal stud.

After paying for her coffee, Ginny walked to the booth and stood there awkwardly with the mug in her hand, waiting for them to shift over to make room for her. Everyone except Dick ignored her presence. He finally gestured magnanimously at a nearby table with empty chairs.

"Pull up a chair!

Ginny clutched one of the spindle-backed chairs—the one with a cushion that looked the most intact—pulled it over to the end of the booth and sat down, but not comfortably. Looking around the room with distress, her gaze was arrested by a table of tough-looking men sitting toward the rear of the room close to an open back door. They were all smoking and laughing drunkenly at something. She forced out several shallow coughs.

"Oh, Jesus," said Harry, rolling his eyes.

"They're not supposed to be smoking inside," Ginny protested, turning back to the table. She was exhausted, and she felt cranky.

Rosie poured herself a glass of beer from the pitcher, and peered at Ginny's coffee. "What's with the java? Don't you drink?"

"Sometimes. Not much. I'm too tired."

Tom was in a good mood. He said, "C'mon. One drink won't kill ya." He poured a foaming glass of beer and shoved it toward her end of the table.

"No, I'm really too tired," she said. Nevertheless, she caught the glass and her fingers began to stroke the wet sides. It was cool to the touch. "When I'm tired like this, I get high too easily. One glass of wine, that's it. Makes me dizzy."

Tom laughed. "My kinda woman—a cheap drunk! C'mon, be sociable. Get dizzy!"

Ginny, remembering that her goal was to show them that she could loosen up, sighed in defeat and began to sip the beer cautiously.

"Where's the boss? Where's Blob?" asked Rosie.

Tom, whose eyes had been darting everywhere, said, "He just came in. He's gettin' his ginger ale at the bar." Turning to Ginny, he said in explanation, "That's the only thing he ever drinks. Ginger ale."

"Ginger ale," repeated Dick. "Bob's beverage of choice. See, Bob, unlike me, is a recovered alcoholic, whereas I..." He lifted one of his shot glasses of vodka high into the air. "...I am an *active* alcoholic! A card-carrying member, and proud of it!" Draining the glass, Dick shoved his chair back and stood unsteadily. "*My name is Dick, and I'm an alcoholic.*"

"Your name is shithead, and you're a fuckin' drunk," retorted Harry, taking a long swig of his beer.

"Yes, that too," replied Dick, falling back heavily into his seat. "So, if I'm a fucking drunk, who is it that I am fucking tonight?" He looked wistfully at Rosie, who crossed her eyes and made a face at him.

Ginny marveled that a human body could tolerate so much alcohol. She was concerned about him. "Haven't you ever wanted to get sober, Dick?" she asked.

"Hell, no. I been a full-fledged alcoholic since I was 14 years old!" he answered proudly. "Before then I was just what they call your heavy drinker."

"Hey, Harry," Tom piped up. "You knew Bob back when he was drinkin'. What was he like? What kinda drunk was he?"

"A mean one," said Harry, pulling out a cigarette and lighting it. Neither the management nor the clientele at Lefty's seemed interested in conforming to the no-smoking rules. Ginny shifted uncomfortably away from the smoke. Harry, well aware of her discomfort, refused to look in her direction.

"You really think the Blob is gonna take time off when his old lady dies?" Tom said.

"Yeah," said Harry, flicking ash onto the floor. "He'll take off."

"No, he won't. The boss *never* takes off work," said Rosie. "If he broke every bone in his body and they put him in a cast, he'd still fucking show up to work. If he caught leprosy, he'd still fucking show up to work."

"He'll take off," repeated Harry with smug assurance. "I know him."

Tom stretched out his arms and cracked his knuckles. "I can't wait. I'm so goddamn sick of him breathin' down our necks, always spyin' on us, checkin' our time cards. Never gives us a goddamn break."

"Shut up. Here comes Mr. Ginger Ale now," said Rosie in a low voice.

"Ginger ale," echoed Tom. Then he looked at Ginny. "Hey, that's *you*! You're Ginny. I hereby name you *Miss Ginny Ale!*"

Bob joined them, holding his soft drink and a blue plastic basket full of pretzels. He pushed the pretzels down the center of the table and pulled up a chair next to Ginny. She realized that he must have showered before coming to the bar. His hair was damp, and he had on a clean blue shirt and jeans. He smelled, as he had that first day, faintly of smoke. It was unlike the tobacco smoke from Harry's cigarette, but instead reminded her of the scent of burning leaves or woodsmoke. She liked it. They were squeezed together so closely that the sleeve of his arm was pressed against hers. Ginny did not feel like pulling away. She was surprised at how comfortable she felt in his physical presence.

"Ginny Ale: a name that is not only a soft drink, but one that is also full of booze. Did you notice that?" proclaimed Dick. "*Ginny*. What a name!" He gestured magnanimously toward her, his voice melodramatic. "I love you. Any woman with booze in her name is a woman I love. Here's to Bloody Mary, here's to Margarita, here's to Brandy—and here's to Ginny Ale!

"Ginny. Where does that come from, anyway? What kinda name is that?" asked Tom amiably.

"It's short for Virginia," she replied.

"Oh, you mean like, 'You make me scrub toilets all the time just 'cause I got a VIRGINIA?'" Rosie shouted gleefully.

The crew laughed boisterously at this. Even Ginny had to smile. Bob, who was slowly nursing his ginger ale, sat back in his chair and watched, the silent observer.

"Well, since we're discussing names," said Ginny, "did you ever realize that you three guys are Tom, Dick, and Harry?" She giggled. She was halfway through her glass of beer, and she was starting to feel it.

"Yeah? So?" said Harry.

"It's a really old expression. You know: *Every Tom, Dick, and Harry*. They always put those three names together."

Harry shrugged.

"When they say '*Every Tom, Dick, and Harry,*' that means everyone," explained Ginny. "It's a saying."

"Never heard it before," said Tom.

"We're fucking famous!" cried Dick. "Like the three musketeers!" He belched loudly.

Tom and Harry immediately followed suit, each trying to outdo one another with successively louder belches. Harry blew smoke rings as he burped. Ginny looked at the three and shook her head.

"Hey, guys, Ginny Ale here ain't happy. You better stop it," said Rosie. Then she let out her own tremendous belch, the loudest of all, and applauded herself.

Ginny smiled tensely and said, "Come on, can you please lay off me?"

"Huh?" said Tom, snapping to attention. "Lay who? Why don't we lay who?"

"What'd *we* do? You're the one who complains all the time," Harry said, crushing his cigarette under his heel.

Ginny retorted, "Is that what you think? That I complain all the time? You know, you're wrong about me. You just don't know me. Sure, I *am* different from you, and yes, I don't like all the things you like. But I'm not that rigid."

"*I* am!" Tom half-rose from his seat. Pretending to unzip his pants, he said to Rosie, "Wanna see?"

Rosie looked at him unenthusiastically. "Lick me."

Tom sat back down. Ginny was still pondering Harry's comment. The beer was having an effect on her, and she spoke more loudly than she normally would have.

"I mean, yes, maybe I have different tastes from you, but that doesn't make me a...a stick in the mud!" she said.

"Sure, I'll lick you," said Tom to Rosie. "You got a different taste, too?"

Harry looked at Ginny. The tattoo of a coiled snake on his right bicep throbbed a little as he clenched his fist.

"Bullshit. People like you, people like *teachers*, you got no life," he sneered. "All you do is go to school, bore the hell outta the kids, go home, and follow your boring rules and regulations." He mimicked her. "'Ooh, you ain't supposed to burp.

Ooh, you ain't supposed to swear. Ooh, why are people smoking in here?" Us, now we ain't afraid to live—to have some fuckin' adventure! Take a big bite outta life!"

Tom made a licking gesture toward Rosie with his tongue. She, in turn, reached for the pretzel basket on the table, picked up a thick pretzel stick, sucked on it briefly, and then, staring at Tom, bit it in half viciously. He winced.

"Oh, adventure is it? So tell me," replied Ginny, draining her glass of beer and setting it firmly down on the table, "is this what you do for adventure? Come to Lefty's? Sit in a booth and drink beer and burp? Do you ever do anything else?"

Dick called out drunkenly, "We make Rosie show us her tit." He turned to Rosie. "Rosie, Rosie, show us your tit!"

Rosie began to comply merrily, reaching for her tank top, but then looked at Bob and stopped.

"Is there anything else you do for adventure?" asked Ginny. A song that had been playing in the background suddenly ended. The table filled with an uncomfortable silence. Ginny spoke again.

"See, you THINK you're risk-takers, but the truth is, you're the ones with the boring lives. Listening to noisy music and talking incessantly about the dimensions of your genitalia—*that* doesn't make you adventurers!"

Rosie gasped and shook her finger disapprovingly. "She said a bad word."

"*Adventurers* is a bad word?" Dick asked in a blurry voice.

"Okay, Ginny Ale, what do you do for excitement that's so great?" said Tom.

"You don't want to know," she replied.

"No, I mean it," he persisted, half-standing to refill Ginny's glass with more beer. "What do you do?"

She took a sip and thought for a moment. "Well, I like to go to concerts. And I go to museums, plays...you know, things like that," replied Ginny.

"Crap, that stuff's not fun," scowled Tom.

"Not fun? Wanna bet? So tell me, when's the last time you went to a museum or saw a play? Any of you?"

There was no response.

"How about this?" she continued loudly. "Since you were all kind enough to invite me to join you tonight, I'll reciprocate."

"Is that something you do that alone, or do you need a partner?" said Tom lustfully. Rosie slapped at his arm.

Ginny ignored them. "I offer you all an open invitation to come along with me to participate in one of the activities I like to do. Any time you choose. You'll have fun. You'll see."

Harry stubbed out a cigarette, crossed his arms and leaned back in the booth. "Sure, right."

"No thanks," yawned Rosie. After she finished yawning, she kept her mouth open and waggled her tongue at Tom. He, in turn, stuck his finger in his mouth and sucked on it, his eyebrows raised in question. Rosie lifted a finger near to her lips, as if to take it in her mouth, and then snapped her teeth ferociously together in the same way she had bitten down on the pretzel, grinning at him.

"What happened to all you risk-takers? asked Ginny. "You're the ones who said you like adventure. C'mon—I dare you to take me up on my invitation!"

Dick stood up. "My name is Dick, and I'm a..." Harry reached to pull him back down, but Dick brushed him away. "... and I'm a RISK TAKER. I'll go with you, Ginny Ale. When are we going?"

Taken by surprise, Ginny thought quickly. "Next Friday after work. Friday is when you guys always get together, presumably to have a good time, right?" A new idea struck her. "Hey, I've got a proposition for you."

"Ginny Ale is propositioning me! Oh baby, I been waitin' to hear that from you! Go ahead," sighed Tom.

"Shut up, Tom," snarled Rosie.

"Here's my proposition: for the rest of the summer—eight weeks left, right?—let me take you all someplace *I* find interesting after work on Friday nights. Just to try something different for a change."

Harry groaned.

"Are you afraid?" she taunted.

"Of what YOU find interesting? Yeah, you bet I am," he glowered, slumping further down in his seat.

Dick tried to pour Ginny a third glass of beer. She covered her glass with her hand, and shook her head.

"No more, thank you, Dick. My head's already spinning."

"Shit," said Tom. "You kidding me? Every Friday night? We ain't in third grade no more. We don't gotta take field trips now, do we?"

"Shut up, you guys," said Rosie, addressing the table. Everyone turned to her. "You know something? I hate to say it, but she's right. We never do *nothin'* when we get together. Okay, I'm in. I'll try it. What's to lose?" She turned to Ginny. "Me an' Dicky'll come."

Tom began to say something, but Rosie glared at him and narrowed her eyes. He sighed in defeat.

"Shit," he said.

Harry then spoke up. "What you want, that's no fuckin' good. You want us to do stuff you like. I say you should take a few risks yourself, and do what *we* find interesting."

Ginny took the challenge. "So tell me: what do you find interesting?"

Harry grimaced. "Not the same crap as you, that's for sure," he said with his arms crossed.

Ginny thought for a moment. "Well, okay, what about this? How about if we alternate? One week I choose what we're going to do on Friday, then the next Friday, you choose."

"That ain't fair!" cried Rosie. "You get every other week. I think we should take equal turns, all of us."

Bob then cleared his throat and, leaning forward, broke his silence. Up until this point he had been listening and watching without expression. "Except that you all like doing the same things, so it's four against one. You guys against Ginny."

He glanced at Ginny, who was startled that he had spoken. She realized that she scarcely knew what his voice sounded like, for he had said little over the past few weeks except to bark out commands.

Bob continued, "Only fair thing is that she chooses what we're gonna do after work on one Friday, the next week one of you chooses, then her, then another one of you, and so on."

Under her breath, Rosie whispered to Harry, "Oh, shit. 'What *we're* gonna do?' He thinks *he's* comin' along?"

Ginny had begun feeling the beers. She said in a voice that was louder than normal, "That sounds good. So first we're going to need to establish some rules."

There were groans from the crew.

"Here we go," said Harry.

"Yes, teacher," said Tom lasciviously. "Tell me the rules. Will you spank me if I'm bad, huh?"

The music began again and surged even more loudly than before. Ginny shouted to make herself heard, the thudding beats punctuating her words. "Okay, listen up. No one can choose an activity that's life-threatening, pornographic, or violent. Or illegal."

"What the hell is left?" said Rosie.

"Damn," joked Tom. "You mean I gotta leave my crack pipe at home?"

Ginny said, "And no sitting in a bar drinking, since we've already done that. It's got to be something different each week."

Dick raised his hand. "Ginny Ale? Can tonight count as my turn, then? 'Cause drinking is the only thing I personally find interesting."

"So who gets next Friday?" said Rosie.

Bob broke his silence again. "Ginny does."

"Where are you gonna take us, Ginny-Ale?" said Dick with a burp. "Will there be alcoholic beverages?"

Ginny smiled triumphantly, as the music stopped and there was once again a momentary hush. "I know exactly where we'll go. I'm going to take you all to...the ballet!"

The crew groaned miserably. Tom knocked with his fist on the underside of the table.

"What's that?" said Ginny.

"Going to the ballet," he replied. "I'm so excited, my hard-on hit the table."

CHAPTER TEN
The Ballet

A WEEK LATER

I T WAS A classical ballet. In contrast to the formal wear of Ginny, who had changed into a flattering blue cocktail dress and high heels, the crew were dressed inappropriately. Along with all her piercings, Rosie wore a dress, but it was a bright orange color, and was both too tight and too short. Tom had on a light hoodie, Dick wore his usual garb—baggy plaid shorts, and Harry sported a black T-shirt and jeans, with his tattoos strongly in evidence. Bob once again wore a clean blue dress shirt; while he looked casual, he at least fit in a little better.

Ginny sat on the aisle with Rosie next to her. There hadn't been enough seats for all six in the same row, so Bob sat behind Ginny. As the ballet began, the crew alternately slouched and squirmed, making it obvious that they were bored. Tom and Harry, a few seats away from Ginny, pulled out candy bars. When Tom unwrapped his, he dropped the wrapper on the floor. Ginny leaned across Rosie's feet to pick it up. Looking insolently at Ginny with narrowed eyes, Harry then tossed his candy wrapper on the floor, deliberately making sure that it was out of her reach. His stare made Ginny shudder. Sometimes he frightened her. She hoped that she would never find herself alone with him.

"God, please, is this ever gonna end?" said Rosie in a stage whisper.

Several people in front of the crew turned around in their seats to hush her. She rolled her eyes in response, and deliberately began to chew her gum too loudly.

The particular ballet that they were watching was finally over. It was the first on a program of several dances, and everyone except the crew applauded politely.

Tom sank further down in his seat like a sulky teenager, his knees higher than his head. "Shit, man, this is really fun," he grumbled.

"Can we go now? I'm thirsty," whined Dick.

Ginny felt as if she were on an outing with her elementary school. "Shhh," she said. "Behave yourselves. There's another dance starting."

The orchestra began playing again, and the audience grew quiet. Rosie stuck her gum on the back of the seat in front of her. Speaking loudly to Harry, she said, "Harry, give me some of your candy."

"Get your own!" he snarled.

"Where? I don't see no snack bar. C'mon, gimme!"

She reached across Tom, who was sitting between them, to grab for Harry's half-eaten candy bar. Harry pulled away. "Don't touch me, you bitch."

A man behind them leaned forward, annoyed. "Shhh," he said.

Rosie whirled to face him in confrontation. Ginny, alarmed, swiftly touched her arm to get her attention, and then raised a warning finger to her lips, shaking her head.

Rosie turned back in her seat, facing front, but she wasn't happy about it. "Yes, Verg-ina," she said with a pout, crossing her legs and arms.

Ginny bristled. "Don't call me that, please. My name is Ginny."

Dick, with slurred excitement, began to rise, proclaiming: "And MY name is DICK, and I'm an alcohol..."

Harry yanked him back down before he could finish.

Fortunately, the people around them didn't notice their last set of antics. The curtain had risen and the audience was applauding as the new ballet began. The music for this dance was tribal, with a strong, powerful drumbeat. Tom started to tap his foot, his head keeping time to the rhythm. Several female dancers leaped onto the stage wearing body stockings. They swayed and stomped to the music in a dance that was both sensual and gymnastic.

"All right! Pussy!" said Tom in a stage whisper, sitting up and craning his neck. Along with Dick and Harry, he began to pay closer attention, while Rosie yawned exaggeratedly and started picking at her teeth. Then a group of male dancers came onstage, wearing similarly skintight attire that revealed bulging crotches and well-muscled arms and legs. Her hand dropped and her mouth hung open.

"Shit," she exclaimed happily, now as equally mesmerized as Tom, Dick, and Harry.

The dance ended in a wild, climactic frenzy of motion, sound, and drums. The crew joined vigorously in the applause. They watched the remaining dances in the program attentively.

As the final curtain fell, Ginny turned to look down the row of seats at them and said, "So—what did you think?"

"I think that calls for a drink," said Dick.

Rosie faked boredom and deliberately yawned again. "Can we please go now?"

"What's on for next Friday?" said Tom.

Bob leaned forward from his seat behind Ginny. She could feel his breath on her cheek. It was not unpleasant.

"Choose something," he said to Tom.

"Okay, boss. I will," grinned Tom.

CHAPTER ELEVEN
Carob and Avocados

SATURDAY

GINNY AND TRACY had made a date to go shopping the day after the ballet. Their first stop was an organic grocery store that Ginny frequented.

As they prowled the aisles, Tracy said, "When you say they were bad at the ballet, how bad do you mean?"

"I'll never be able to go back there unless I disguise myself," groaned Ginny. "Remember two years ago, that field trip to the planetarium, when we had to send the entire fifth grade home?"

"That bad?" exclaimed Tracy. "Wow."

"Worse!" said Ginny.

"So why didn't you do what we did with the kids at the planetarium, and send them all home?

"I should never have had those beers," Ginny sighed. "That's what started it all."

Tracy picked up a wrapped brownie, ready to add it to the empty shopping cart she was pushing.

Ginny reached out a hand to stop her. "You don't want that. It's not chocolate. It's carob."

Tracy quickly put the dessert back.

"Yeccch. How can you eat this stuff?" she exclaimed.

As they moved further down the aisle, Tracy said, "Hey, speaking of chocolate, I need to get off my rear end more. Or maybe..." she patted her ample bottom, "get more of my rear end off."

Ginny laughed.

"Anyway, it's time for this gorgeous body of mine to start burning calories. Want to get together and take a walk with me tomorrow morning?"

"Sounds good, but I'll be at church," Ginny said. "I'm singing tomorrow." She had a beautiful voice, and often sang solos in her church.

They moved to the produce area where Ginny began inspecting the avocados. Glancing over her shoulder to make sure that no other shoppers were nearby, she lowered her voice and said, "Do you know what they've started calling me, Tracy? They're calling me Vergina...as in vagina. Can you believe it?"

"The PRESBYTERIANS call you that?" said Tracy in astonishment, bring her shopping cart to a halt.

"No," laughed Ginny. "The guys at the park."

"So at least they're actually talking to you now," said Tracy. "That's an improvement, right?"

Ginny frowned at the dark green fruit in her hand. "I'm not so sure about that."

CHAPTER TWELVE
Church

❦

SUNDAY

GOING TO CHURCH was a welcome relief for Ginny after working all week with the crew. Her views were more spiritual than religious, but the church and its timeless rituals made her feel somehow secure and comfortable. They in turn were grateful to have her as a soloist

When it was time for the offertory, she rose from a pew in the chancel and moved forward to the lectern to sing, wearing an ivory-colored choir robe. She had a pretty, lilting soprano voice, the kind of pleasant voice that nearly everybody liked. This morning she sang an arrangement of an old-fashioned hymn called *This Is My Father's World*:

This is my Father's world, and to my
listening ears
All nature sings, and round me rings
The music of the spheres.

This is my Father's world; I rest me in the
thought
Of rocks and trees, of skies and seas,
His hand the wonders wrought.

This is my Father's world; the birds their
carols raise,
The morning light, the lily white,
Declare their Maker's praise.

This is my Father's world; He shines in all
that's fair;
In the rustling grass I hear Him pass,
He speaks to me everywhere.

She sang the familiar tune as the ushers moved down the aisles passing the collection plates, her voice echoing sweetly in the high arching rafters of the sanctuary. Toward the end of the song, sunlight broke through a stained glass window of Jesus holding a lamb, bathing the congregation in pools of colored light. Ginny closed her eyes reverently during the last stanza of the hymn.

When she opened them, to her surprise she saw Bob sitting toward the back of the congregation. He was enveloped in a radiant blue light that was streaming off stained glass, and he was watching her intently. Their eyes met and held for a moment.

It felt as if the man she knew from the park had only been a shell, and she was seeing Bob, the real Bob, for the first time. She felt a surreal sense of connection, and her heart beat a little faster.

After the church service ended, Ginny got out of her choir robe as quickly as she could, hurriedly gathering up her music from the organist who had accompanied her, and rushed to the street. When she got outdoors, Bob was still in view, although he was already far down the sidewalk that led to the parking lot. She ran after him.

"Bob! Bob Corbett! Wait up!" she called.

He turned, saw her, and stopped. As Ginny caught up to him, he resumed walking. Trotting at his side, she felt a little rush of excitement.

"I didn't know you were Presbyterian," she exclaimed.

"I'm not," he replied gently.

"Oh. So what church do you belong to?"

Bob looked down at a little red anthill that had erupted in one of the pavement cracks. He carefully avoided stepping on it.

"None," he answered.

"So what were you doing here in my church then?"

"Just visiting," he replied, still looking down.

Ginny felt distraught by his laconic communication, but something made her persist. "Do you have friends that go here? Maybe I know them...."

"No."

Despite his terse answers, he didn't seem to mind her questions, and it was easy to walk at his side, Bob's stride and hers slipping into a natural rhythm. She looked up at him questioningly. He glanced at her for a moment, and she was startled by the depth in his eyes.

"Sometimes I just feel like visiting different churches," he said finally in explanation, focusing on the sidewalk again. "Last week I went to a Quaker meeting. Week before that, I went to a synagogue."

"Wow, how ecumenical you are," Ginny said.

Bob didn't seem to understand the word. He shrugged.

"That must be interesting," she continued. "Are you trying to find a church that you like so that you can join?"

"No," Bob said. The hint of a smile crossed his lips, as if the question was ridiculous.

"You mean you visit all these different churches, but you don't want to join any of them? That's strange."

"How so?" he asked. "Last I heard, God hadn't joined a church yet. Why should I?"

They came to the entrance of the parking lot and, giving her a friendly goodbye wave, Bob walked to his truck. Ginny watched him with a puzzled expression on her face.

CHAPTER THIRTEEN
A New Realization

❦

MONDAY MORNING

AFTER HER CONVERSATION with Bob the day before, Ginny realized that she was strangely eager to go to work. She felt a little bit let down when she arrived at the shed on her bicycle and saw that his truck wasn't there yet.

As she and the crew put on their coveralls, Tom, pulling up one leg of his pants, began to grunt and fumble loudly.

"Whatsa matter with you now?" asked Harry.

"Damn cock of mine," said Tom. "Too fuckin' long. Gets in the way. I always gotta adjust it. Runs straight down my leg."

Rosie was zipping up the top of her coveralls.

Dick called out, "Rosie, Rosie, show us your tit. Pop my eyes open an' cure my hangover."

Rosie, bored, partially unzipped her coveralls and flashed a bare breast at them. Tom stared, big-eyed, at her breast. His leg stiffly began to rise in the air.

"See? What'd I tell ya?" said Tom.

Ginny was in a good mood. Despite herself, she giggled.

"My balls got names. I named them," said Dick proudly.

"Oh, yeah? What—Shrimpy and Shorty?" laughed Rosie, stuffing her breast back into her top and her coveralls.

"The one on the right is Mo," proclaimed Dick. "Curly is on the left...and SPIKE is in the middle."

"I bet they got a neighbor who's a real asshole," cracked Tom, grinning at his own joke.

"I got names for mine, too," growled Harry.

"Whaddya call yours?" said Rosie, pulling her hair back and fastening it with a gaudy clip.

Harry made a face of scorn. "Ball, ball and prick." He pulled out a cigarette and tried to light it, but even after repeated tries, his lighter wouldn't work. "This one's shot. Anybody got a light?"

Rosie went to her purse, pulled out a red plastic lighter, and handed it to him.

"What's this? Your crack lighter?" He clicked on it, and the end burst into a large flame. He jumped back. "Jesus," he cried. After lighting his cigarette, Harry handed the lighter back to her. She pushed his hand away.

"Nah, keep it. I didn't buy it," she said.

"You been shoplifting lighters again, Rosie?"

"So what if I did?" she said defensively. "That ain't nothin' compared to all the shit you done."

Ginny was not eager to hear what Harry had done. To her relief, Bob entered before he could reply. Her heart jumped a little when she saw him. She immediately squelched the sensation and told herself there was no reason for her to get excited.

Bob, striding over to check the time cards, glanced at Harry's cigarette. "Out. Now," he said, his jaw clenched.

With a sullen expression on his face, Harry crushed the cigarette underfoot on the floor, while Bob studied the time cards laboriously. As he scrutinized them, Tom began tapping his leg.

"Driving's a bitch, you know," he said. "Gets in the way when I wanna slam on the brakes. But the worst thing? It's when I take a pee. Pulling it all the way out, tucking it all the way back in..." He gave a heavy sigh.

"Is that why your shoes always smell like you pissed in 'em?" retorted Rosie.

Once again Ginny was unable to suppress a giggle. Her laughter, however, was caught short as Bob suddenly and angrily slammed the time cards on his desk. Startled, she let out a little gasp of surprise.

"Dick, you were five minutes late. AGAIN."

He spoke to the rest of the crew, and he grew more furious with each word.

"Look, I let you guys settle in and get dressed *after* you punch the time clock, not before. You do a whole hell of a lot more goofing off than you should. It's on my time, my dime, and I don't say anything. But this is not a charity. Harry, you keep on smoking indoors next to all this fuel, you're OUTTA here! Dick, you keep on being late, you're OUTTA here! That goes for ALL of you!"

Bob stormed out of the shed, slamming the door behind him.

Ginny was shaken by the vehemence of Bob's outburst, especially after his laid-back geniality only the day before.

Rosie made a face. "Speaking of big pricks," she muttered.

"What's with him?" said Tom.

"I came in yesterday afternoon to try to fix that broken mower with him," said Harry. "I heard him on the phone before I left. His mother got worse."

"So me 'n you's gonna get fired just 'cause an old lady's sick? Shit," said Dick.

Rosie cried, "She better not fuckin' die, not yet. That goddamn money is *mine!*"

"I'm confused," said Ginny. "Why are you taking bets about when Bob's mother dies? What do you care? Isn't that cruel?"

"Oh God, here we go again," muttered Rosie.

Dick took a noisy swig from the vodka bottle that he had pulled out of its hiding place after Bob left, went to Ginny, and put his arm sloppily around her shoulder. She carefully lifted it off. He was more intoxicated than usual.

"See, Ginny Ale, when she dies, we get us a vacation, 'cause the old slave driver'll take off for a bunch of days," he said, his voice slurred.

"Yeah. Harry'll be in charge," chimed in Tom. "And when that happens, we're not gonna do any fucking work at all. Right, Harry?" Tom shoved Harry in the shoulder as he spoke. In response, Harry gave him a backhanded smack on the thigh.

Tom clutched his still-stiff leg with both arms and began hopping around as if he were in pain.

"Watch it, pervert," he said to Harry.

Ginny continued her questioning. "What's the big deal? Bob doesn't hang around where we work half the time anyhow."

"Oh, you wanna bet?" cried Rosie, her voice suddenly shrill. "He spies on us! And if he's in a bad mood and he drives past and he thinks you ain't workin' hard enough, he'll fire you. He *will*." She turned to the crew. "Remember how he fired McFarland right out of the blue that day?"

They all grunted in agreement.

Dick took another generous drink. "And the thing is, where else is any one of us gonna get another job? In case you haven't figured it out, Ginny Ale, you are working with a bunch of unemployable losers. Take Harry," he said. "Harry's done hard time..."

"Shut up," snarled Harry.

"Rosie's a ho..." he continued

Rosie leapt to her feet. "Hey, hey, you shitfaced liar—I never once done it for money! I do it for *free*."

Grinning, Tom stepped to Rosie's side and pointed to his leg, raising his eyebrows in question.

"Me, I'm a drunk," said Dick, "and Tom—well, Tom's just too fucking stupid to find work anyplace else. He's...what'dya call it? Mentally handicapped."

Tom tapped his leg. "Physically. *Physically*."

Harry started to exit, and then turned back to Dick. "Dick, you got the truck keys?"

Dick took the keys out of his pocket and deftly tossed them up into the air, but he wasn't sober enough to catch them.

"Wait a minute. You're going to let Dick drive?" Ginny asked.

"Why not?" said Harry in a threatening voice.

"Because he's been drinking," she said.

"He's *always* drinkin'," said Rosie.

"Well today he's been drinking more," said Ginny. She turned to Dick and repeated, "You've been drinking."

"SURPR-I-I-ISE!" shouted Dick, holding up both arms in the air and waggling his hands and fingers.

He forgot he had the keys in his hand, and they dropped to the floor again. Dick crouched down to get them. He moved to the area where Ginny was sitting, and attempted to look up between her legs.

"That's not safe. Someone in his condition should not drive," she protested, pulling her legs together.

"Shit, man, Dick *always* drives. Don't be such a tightass," said Harry, exiting. The crew prepared to follow him.

"He's our rock 'n roll leader!" said Tom, moving toward the door.

"I never done it for money, never," said Rosie, coming off the table where she had flopped herself down. "God, is it Friday yet?" she continued wearily. "I wish it was Friday."

"Hey, you guys wanna known what we're doin' after work on Friday? 'Cause Friday's *my* turn," Tom said proudly.

"What?" asked Rosie.

"I'll give you a clue. It's got somethin' to do with balls, and a big hard stick, and getting to home base, and it's one of my favorite activities!"

Ginny followed them out the door and watched, perturbed, as Dick climbed into the driver's seat of the truck with the pint of vodka tucked into the back pocket of his coveralls. The rest of the crew clambered, laughing, into the rear of the truck. Ginny remained standing in the driveway, her brows furrowed.

"You coming?" Rosie called down to her.

"Dick should not be driving," she said. "Where's Bob?"

Harry leaned over the side of the truck to reply. "The Blob's gone over to check out the basketball courts. Anyhow, he don't care."

Ginny stood her ground. It was not easy for her to do. Harry exuded a meanness that she did not want to trigger. "Drunk drivers cause accidents. They kill people."

"He kills *me!*" joked Tom. "C'mon, Vergina, get in. Where's that sense of adventure you're always yapping about?

"There's a difference between taking a risk and being a fool. I'll ride my bike," she said, grim-lipped.

Rosie turned to the crew. "We're risk-takers, she's a fool. Did I get it right?"

"You know how far away it is to where we're working today? Almost ten miles," said Tom, with a slight look of concern. "The boss'll be mad if he comes by and you're not there yet."

Ginny began to unlock her bicycle. "I don't care. I refuse to ride with a drunk."

"Have it your way," shrugged Tom.

"Tight-assed cunt," mumbled Rosie. Ginny heard her and knew that Rosie had intended to be overheard.

The truck squealed off with a chorus of yowling cheers.

Ginny began pedaling to the park site. The first part of the journey was uphill, and in only a few minutes she was breathing heavily and sweating. After a while, her legs started to feel as though they were made from concrete. To worsen the situation, it began to rain. She pushed forward stubbornly as the drops of water slashed at her face, as though slapping her in punishment for having had expectations about Bob, for her thoughts had turned to him.

"What was I thinking?" she said to herself. "That just because we had a little conversation, he was suddenly going to ask me out on a date? That he was going to turn into a normal, courteous man? If he were a normal, courteous man, he would have said something to me about my solo yesterday."

While it wasn't necessary for Ginny to be complimented on her singing, she had begun to brood a little bit about the fact that he hadn't even commented on it. Did it mean that he didn't like her voice? Nearly anyone else would have at least mentioned her solo. There had admittedly been something pleasantly engaging about their conversation, but she realized now that hoping to get to know Bob in a normal boy-girl sense, much less expecting him to exhibit normal courtesy, was the equivalent of believing that he would ride up on a white horse and sweep her away. It wasn't going to happen.

As she pedaled in the rain, her thoughts turned to Rosie's words: *Tight-assed cunt.* The taunt bothered her, and it was even more painful because it had come from another female. Rosie, she thought, should want to be an ally of hers, not an enemy.

Squinting against the rain and feeling more miserable with every minute, she wondered how long she could keep on working with Bob and the crew. The end of summer was still a long way off.

The road finally became level and she was able to coast for a few minutes. As she did so, a new realization struck her.

"The only reason I'm still working with these people is because of the money," she mused. "And good grief, it's *only* money. I am a free woman, after all. Yes, I'm a little broke right now, but it's not like I'm a slave. I have another job waiting for me in a few months, my *real* job. The park doesn't own me. Nobody is depending on me. Bills or no bills, I'm not locked into a contract. I could quit tomorrow if I wanted to."

The thought of quitting made her smile. It came to her that she could and she *would* quit any time she'd had enough, and that time might come very soon. With this heady revelation, she took a deep and satisfied breath. A new sense of empowerment swept over her as she pedaled more vigorously toward the park.

CHAPTER FOURTEEN
Play Ball!

THE NEXT FRIDAY

GINNY DIDN'T QUIT. She showed up for work as usual throughout the week. After the insights she'd gotten on the bike, she felt a renewed freedom that made it easier for her to ignore the insults and crudeness of the crew, and to squelch the fleeting attraction that she had begun to have for Bob.

Tom seemed to grow excited as Friday approached. He had eagerly chosen baseball for the activity that they would engage in after work, and he brought it up multiple times during the week. After Ginny's confrontation with the crew about Dick's drunk driving, she did not look forward to socializing with them. Since the Friday outings had been her idea, however, she decided to go along to the game, albeit reluctantly.

Bob had worked alone for the entire week, only stopping in briefly to check the time cards and to give the group their assignments, so it was a surprise when he showed up at the end of the day on Friday to find out where they were going to gather. Tom happily directed everyone to grab some food and then to meet in a nearby field with short, dry grass that stood next to a used-car lot.

The crew were already there by the time Ginny arrived. Tom and Harry were busy setting up an improvised baseball diamond.

"How come we ain't using a ball field in one of the parks?" called out Rosie as she tested the weight of the bat.

Before Tom could reply, Bob, who had just gotten out of his truck, said, "Little League and local teams take up all the fields on Fridays. They pay rent."

His presence helped to even out the game.

"Okay, you guys, we got two teams," announced Tom, enjoying his role as boss. "Rosie, Harry, Bob— you're on the blue team. Me and Dick and Ginny Ale are on the red team."

As they began, Ginny, who hadn't played baseball since seventh-grade gym class, was instructed by Tom to stand out in the field with him while Dick pitched.

The first up to bat was Rosie. She swung at the ball three times and missed.

"You're out!" cried Tom jubilantly.

"Dicky is throwin' curve balls," she yelled.

"That, ma'am, is the advantage of having a drinking man do your pitching," replied Dick, tugging at the baseball cap he had donned for the occasion and taking a deep bow.

Harry strode over to Rosie, snatched the bat away from her, hit the ball easily on the first pitch, and raced toward first base. Tom charged after the ball, picked it up, and threw it hard at Harry, managing to tag him out, while Ginny stood by helplessly. Harry walked off the field in disgust.

It was Bob's turn to bat next. On the first pitch, he hit a home run. The ball bounced off the roofs of the battered cars in the lot next door.

"Attaway, boss! *Now* we're playin'!" screamed Rosie. She stepped up to home plate again, doing a triumphant little dance step, as Harry ran to fetch the baseball.

Tom called out, "Rosie, Rosie, show us your tit!"

Rosie, grasping the bat in one hand, obligingly pulled a breast out of her top and then quickly tucked it in again, glancing at Bob. He was still busy taking his victory lap around the bases and didn't notice. On the first pitch, Rosie hit the ball high into the air and began running.

"No fair, no fair! She distracted the pitcher," cried Dick. "Where the hell is the umpire?"

Rosie's ball began to drop down from the sky in a gentle arc directly above Ginny. Instead of catching it, however, she instinctively covered her face with her arm and ducked. The ball fell down next to her and began to roll along the ground. She stumbled clumsily after it, reaching repeatedly but unable to grasp it. Her teammates watched her with open-mouthed dismay.

"Jesus fuckin' Christ!" exclaimed Tom.

Finally he raced over to Ginny's side. He snatched the ball and tackled Rosie with it just as she was leaving third base and running toward home, knocking her to the ground. He lay on top of her and remained there much longer than necessary, thoroughly enjoying himself.

"Sorry," sighed Ginny, apologizing to no one in particular. "I'm not very coordinated when it comes to sports...."

The teams traded places. Bob was elected pitcher for the other team. He was a good pitcher, and threw swift, aggressive pitches at both Tom and Dick, pitilessly striking them out. When Ginny came to bat, she tried her best to act spunky, but it was obvious by the awkward way in which she held the bat that she was painfully inept. Bob pitched much less ruthlessly to her than to the men. Swinging wildly, she still missed connecting with the ball. Shaking his head, Bob trotted over to her.

"I'm sorry," Ginny said again. "I'm really not very good at sports."

"Can I show you?" asked Bob.

Ginny nodded.

Bob called out to the others, "Time out."

"Race you to the water," shouted Tom.

With a whoop, he and the crew began to race one another boisterously to the edge of the field where there was a case of bottled water. As he, Dick, and Harry engaged in shoving each other out of the way, Rosie ran ahead of them and declared herself the winner. The three men joined her, and they gleefully began to splash one another with sprays of water.

While they horsed around, Bob drew nearer to Ginny and demonstrated how to hold the bat. He stood behind her, but he kept his body almost unnaturally pulled away from her to avoid the old cliché of the man teaching the woman by wrapping his arms around her. Nevertheless, his hands touched hers as he readjusted her grip, and lingered for a fraction of a second longer than they should have.

When Ginny turned her head around to say something to him, she was startled to find his lips and face only a few inches from hers. A fleeting but almost palpable moment of attraction passed between them which took Ginny by surprise. They both seemed embarrassed by this and swiftly separated. Ginny covered the awkwardness of the moment by giving out a nervous giggle. Bob began to chuckle as well, and soon, standing side by side, they were both laughing.

The crew then came charging back, drenched and ready to resume the game. Bob, still smiling, started to return to the pitcher's mound. He stopped walking when he was only halfway there. Turning around, he threw the ball gently to Ginny in a slow underhand pitch. She struck at it with her bat, but she still missed.

"Strike two," shrieked Rosie.

"Hey, you're too close. That's not fuckin' fair!" yelled Harry.

Bob eyed him steadily. "If you're jealous, Harry, I'm sure Dick will be more than happy to pitch like this to you."

"Yeah," chimed in Rosie. "Maybe then you'll actually be able to get a run, Harry."

Bob turned his attention back to Ginny. On the second underhanded pitch he threw, she connected with the ball. It soared high into the air. With a surprised squeal of delight, she began to run.

Tom turned proudly to Dick. "Did'cha see that? I think our little Vergina has hit a home run!"

Meanwhile, Harry ambled easily to the middle of the field. With his eyes disdainfully on Ginny, he reached up effortlessly with a gloved hand and caught the ball.

CHAPTER FIFTEEN
Jumping into the Pool

THE FOLLOWING WEDNESDAY

TRACY WAS STILL on her exercise kick, and had begged both Ginny and Beth to join her for a water aerobics class at the local YMCA. She got the starting time wrong, however, so the trio arrived early and had the pool to themselves for a while. Tracy and Beth plunged into the water immediately and began paddling placidly back and forth, while Ginny squatted on the sidelines, splashing herself as she worked up the courage to jump in. She wore a modest blue one-piece bathing suit.

"Sounds to me like you're getting a little thing for this boss of yours," said Beth, wiping her curly wet hair back from her forehead and exchanging a knowing glance with Tracy as she tread water.

"No," replied Ginny with a shake of her head, her lips firm. "Absolutely no."

"Do you like his looks?" asked Beth.

"That has nothing whatsoever to do with it," Ginny said. She sat down on the ledge of the pool and dangled her feet in the water, kicking aimlessly.

"Oh, come on. Do you? Do you think he's nice looking?" persisted Beth.

"Okay," said Ginny reluctantly, "yeah, I guess I find him sort of attractive in a rough-looking kind of way, but...."

Beth smiled smugly and nodded at Tracy. "Told you."

Ginny paused. "He's black," she said soberly.

After another moment of silence, Beth said, "So is that a problem for you?"

"Well, it doesn't make it easy," said Ginny. She changed her posture then and began to slide into the water. "Anyway, nothing is going to happen. I mean, we've scarcely even spoken to one another."

OVER THE COURSE of their several weeks of working together, except for their brief conversation after church that one day and the recent baseball lesson, the only real contact they'd had was that their eyes had met now and then, and their bodies had accidentally brushed together a few times. Those incidents weren't anything that she was about to share with her friends. She'd had enough life experience to realize that a little eye and body contact didn't count for much, especially with Bob's tendency to distance himself. As soon as she would begin to think that they might be getting closer—that something might be starting—he would always pull away, so she had concluded that it would be best to try to keep her feelings in check.

Earlier that week, for instance, she had the job of planting flowers in East Park, replacing some of the wilted pansies with hardier blooms that would last until the first frost. Ginny enjoyed working that day. Bob had elected to plant flowers with her, and for once the rest of the crew were out of sight and sound, cleaning the playground and barbecue pits at the other end of the park. The sky was a deep clear blue, with only a few random clouds floating slowly by, and the temperature was perfect, pleasantly warm without being too hot. A gentle breeze kept the bugs away, and a bird she could not identify serenaded them with rich, happy warbles.

The flower beds ran on both sides of the walking path. As she knelt, digging with her trowel, Bob was busy planting on the opposite side. Their backs were to each other. At one point, she felt a strong awareness of him. Looking over her shoulder, she found him staring at her. Their eyes met. It made Ginny flush, because in the moments before she had sensed his energy, she had been thinking about him. Bob seemed flustered as well, and immediately shifted his eyes away.

Later that day, as she was raking around the flower beds, enjoying the scents of the earth and the spicy-sweet smell of the blossoms, she saw him trying to drag a park bench to a new location near a fountain. It was long and he was struggling to balance it by himself. Ginny dropped her rake and quietly stepped over to pick up the other end of the bench. Bob seemed startled when he realized that it was she who was helping him. Their eyes met momentarily once again; then, moving in smooth coordination, they carried the bench together to its new destination.

The only other contact they'd had during the week was just as subtle, and it had happened on the following day. The entire crew were busy trimming trees. Harry and Bob were high in the trees with chainsaws, cutting away dead wood. The others stood on the ground, pulling the largest branches with ropes as they fell to make sure that they landed in the right place. Everyone was focused on a particularly heavy branch when a hard storm came up behind them, taking them by surprise. Rain suddenly began to fall. Whooping, the crew galloped away from the pelting drops of water and took shelter under a picnic area near them that had a roof. Ginny, laughing helplessly, stumbled after them, her clothes almost instantly soaked and rain streaming down her neck.

Once she reached the shelter, she felt observed. She turned around to see Bob, who had climbed down from the tree. He was standing in the rain, watching her, holding the chainsaw limply in one hand. As soon as she spotted him, he pretended to be looking at something else...or perhaps he had been looking at something else all along, and she had just imagined that he was staring at her.

Regardless of what had caught his attention, for a few moments he didn't seem to realize that he was getting wet. When it suddenly struck him, he raced for the shelter, and sat down at a picnic table next to Tom and Harry to wait out the storm. The three became engaged in conversation, but Ginny couldn't hear what they were saying; their words were drowned out by the pounding roar of the rain on the shelter's metal roof. Bob continued to cast covert glances at Ginny as they talked. She wasn't sure that his glances meant much. Her coveralls were sturdy and unattractive, and it wasn't as if she had a wet T-shirt on. She finally decided that Bob kept looking at her because of how ridiculous her rain-soaked hair must have looked, sticking out from her head in silly clumps.

GINNY SIGHED, STILL kicking at the water in the pool. "The man can scarcely even read," she said. She felt a twinge of guilt as she spoke, as if she were betraying him, but she continued anyway. "People like Bob are the reason literacy coalitions get started. He probably thinks good grammar is a—a sweet old lady who bakes cookies."

"Ginny, sometimes you crack me up," laughed Tracy.

Beth persisted with her questions. "What about his personality? Don't you like his personality?" she said.

"Ah. That's another thing," replied Ginny sourly. "He has none. He picks on the crew, he's sullen, he's rude, he never comes to my defense when they turn on me, which is all the time. He's obviously not on anything close to my cultural or intellectual level..."

"Hmmm," mused Beth. "Sounds to me like you've been thinking a lot about him."

"Beth, he works in a park, for gosh sakes! He's the equivalent of a school janitor, except that he works outdoors!" protested Ginny. She continued to feel uncomfortable talking about Bob in this way. She was seldom unkind, and her words were leaving a bad taste in her mouth.

"So do you. You work outdoors, too," said Tracy."

"Yes, but not by choice," Ginny replied.

"Since when did a person's resume or SAT scores figure into body chemistry anyhow?" said Beth.

"Attraction isn't only about physical chemistry. I like brains. Smart men turn me on."

"How come?" asked Beth. "Look at the way men are. Politicians, businessmen, even Rhodes Scholars: they go for bimbos all the time. The more powerful they are, the more they seem to need some brainless beauty on their arm. So why not reverse that, and let yourself be on the arm of a brainless guy?"

Ginny squirmed uncomfortably. "I didn't exactly mean he was brainless. Can we talk about something else, please?" she pleaded.

"No, not yet," continued Beth. "I've got a plan. Here's what I think you should do. I think you ought to seduce this guy...what's his name again?"

Ginny and Tracy said his name at the same time: "Bob."

"I think you ought to seduce this Bob and have a wild affair—just long enough for him to work on your car and repair all the stuff that's broken around the apartment. That's what dumb guys were created for. Use 'em, and after everything's fixed— and of course after you've had all the sex you want— then dump 'em."

Tracy laughed. Ginny tried to join her, but she couldn't get away from a nagging guilt at the entire conversation.

"Now you're sounding like the crew at work," she mumbled.

Tracy nudged Beth and said, "They call her *Vergina*."

Beth giggled as Ginny, holding her nose, finally jumped into the pool.

When she bobbed her head up, Beth was still giggling.

"It's really not so enchanting, Beth, being called the name of an intimate body part. It's embarrassing," she said. "And Bob's not dumb," she added.

"You guys still doing the Friday thing?" asked Tracy.

"Yes. Who knows why."

"Where are you going to go this week?" said Tracy.

Ginny replied, "It's my turn. They claimed they needed something more physical, so we're going to go bike riding on that trail that runs along the river."

CHAPTER SIXTEEN
The Bike Ride

❧

THE NEXT FRIDAY NIGHT

T HE BIKE TRAIL where they met looped around the outskirts of the city, running along the side of a winding river. It was one of Ginny's favorite places to ride, being both paved and, in places, wide. Large sections of the trail were surrounded by wild areas where woods gradually gave way to marshes and tall reeds. Other parts of the trail bordered civilization. The whole route was infused with the smells of the river.

Everyone except Ginny rode on a bike that had been rented from a shop at the head of the trail. She had brought her own bicycle, and she was the only one wearing a helmet.

The late afternoon was warm. As they pedaled away from the rental shop, Ginny congratulated herself on choosing bike riding. She hoped it would be just demanding enough to give the crew something to do with their energy so that they couldn't misbehave too wildly.

'If I remember to treat them like my third-graders," she thought, "things might go well."

Dick pulled out to the front of the pack. It had obviously been a while since he had ridden a bike. He struggled for balance, wobbling nearly out of control.

"Hey, asshole," shouted Tom, "why didn't you rent some training wheels for that thing?"

"Thirsty," Dick called back to him. "I need a drink to steady me, that's all. I'm too sober."

Rosie had rented a bike with a basket, and she had placed her speaker in it. Several minutes into the ride, she turned on the music. A sudden blast of earsplitting rap ripped through the air. Ginny pulled up alongside of her and shouted to be heard above the noise.

"Sorry, but no," said Ginny. "Today it's *my* turn— remember?"

Rosie reluctantly turned the music off and under her breath muttered, "Bitch."

"Come off it, Rosie," said Ginny, trying not to let the other's sulkiness destroy her mood. "Don't you see, part of this is listening to the birds, and watching the river, and feeling the peacefulness of the..." Rosie rolled her eyes and Ginny stopped. "Forget it," she said.

As the foliage grew thicker, Tom, showing off, shot ahead of everybody and then circled back toward them, raising his hands over his head and waving his long fingers.

"Lookee! No hands!" he cried.

His bike veered suddenly and crashed into a thicket where, to the enormous amusement of the crew, he was thrown to the ground. He lay face down, motionless. Ginny immediately jumped off her bike and ran to his side, bending over him with concern. The others drew up to watch.

"Tom? Tom? Are you okay?" she asked.

She gently touched his shoulder. He didn't move. One of his legs seemed to be twisted at a strange angle.

"Lookee," crowed Rosie. "No more Tom."

Ginny was concerned. She leaned down more closely. "I think maybe he's hurt," she said.

Tom suddenly turned over with a grin and lunged at her with both arms, dragging her down salaciously on top of him. She shrieked and pulled quickly away. The crew thought that this was hilarious.

When they mounted their bikes and took off down the trail again, before they gained distance from one another Dick called out, "Somethin' familiar about this place."

"You've been here before, but in winter, when they shift us over to county," replied Bob, who was in the center of the pack. "This is a county path. We don't spend a lot of time here."

"Yeah, we been here before with the trail snowplow," added Harry. He seemed to be enjoying the ride.

His pedal accidentally brushed against Rosie's foot. "Sorry. Pardon me," he said courteously. He slowed and fell to the back with an uncharacteristic smile on his face.

Rosie pedaled faster and caught up to Tom. Ginny, who was only slightly ahead of them, heard their conversation.

"Hey, Tom," Rosie said in a muted voice. "What the fuck is wrong with Harry? He just acted polite!"

"Gotta be stoned," said Tom offhandedly.

Ginny turned to look back at them, and spoke softly so that she would not be overhead. "Does Harry do that? Take drugs?"

Tom looked at Ginny with some amazement and replied, "Does a cow crap manure?"

"How would you know?" cried Rosie. "You never seen no cow!"

He looked over at her. "Sure I have. Lotsa times."

"Where?" Rosie said. "And if you say you're lookin' at one now, wave goodbye to your nuts."

Tom sat up tall. "I seen a cow every time I eat a hamburger."

He grinned at Rosie, and she stuck her tongue out at him. Ginny, not wanting to hear any more, pulled out further ahead of them. A short time later, Tom broke away from Rosie's side and began to catch up to Ginny. Riding directly behind her bike, he stared with exaggerated appreciation at her rear end. Dick rode up as well, and crowded close to Tom to get him to fall back. The trail had narrowed, and in this section it was barely wide enough for the two bikes.

"Yo, Tom, move!" shouted Dick. "I wanna ride behind Vergina!"

"No way. Get the hell out. *I* wanna ride behind Vergina!"

"Hey, why don't nobody want to ride behind me?" Rosie cried out loudly.

"Everybody's already ridden *your* behind, Rosie," hollered Harry from the rear, "but nobody's tried Vergina yet." There was a nasty undertone in Harry's voice that made Ginny shudder.

They continued down the path, and the sun began to set, casting a magical golden haze over the trees and shrubs. Tom started to sing absently to himself. His tenor voice had a polished, mellow sound. Ginny, mesmerized, stopped pedaling for a moment and coasted back to get closer to him.

"Wow, Tom," she said in surprise. "You've got a gorgeous voice. You're really good!"

Tom immediately stopped singing and looked embarrassed. For once, he didn't know what to say.

Dick, calling from behind Tom, whined, "Vergina! When are you gonna let us take a break?"

"I mean it," said Ginny, ignoring Dick. "You have a gift."

"When I was a kid, I always thought I'd like to take voice lessons some day," said Tom. After a moment, he added cautiously, "So you teach people how to sing, right? You give voice lessons?"

"I've done that," she said, nodding. Spotting a grassy patch ahead, she pointed at it and called back to the crew. "Let's break here, guys."

In a hesitant voice, Tom said, "Would you ever consider, like, giving me a singing lesson?"

They came to a halt, and the crew pulled up behind them just in time to hear her reply, "I'll do it whenever you want, Tom. Any time at all. Simply say the word."

Harry and Dick erupted in shouts and guffaws, while Rosie glared jealously at Tom. Exchanging their usual lewd comments about Ginny's remark, the crew sprawled comfortably on the grass with their bicycles strewn next to them. Overhead, the clouds were gradually changing color, from a deep rust to purples and pinks. Ginny found herself sitting on the grass next to Bob. She removed her helmet and tried to fluff out her hair. This was followed by an awkward silence between the two that she finally broke.

"Nice afternoon," she said. "No mosquitoes."

"Yes," he replied, not meeting her eyes.

Ginny cleared her throat shyly, unable to think of more to say. Then she became aware of a faint humming sound in the background. Rosie, hearing it as well, lifted herself on one elbow and, looking around for the source of the noise, spotted something on a branch a few yards distant.

"Oh, shit!" She scrambled to her feet and began to back away nervously.

"What the fuck's wrong with you?" growled Harry.

Rosie pointed wordlessly. Hanging from the branch was what looked like a large brown football-shaped balloon. It was a huge swarm of bees, clustered tightly together. As the others realized this, all of them except for Bob jumped up and dashed nervously away. He rose and walked right over to the bees.

"Don't worry," he said calmly. "They won't attack. They're swarming...looking for a new home. Usually bees only attack when they have a hive to defend. If I had a box with me, I could probably break the branch right off and put the whole swarm in it without getting stung."

Shuddering, Rosie cried, "Why would anybody wanna carry a bunch of bees away in a box, if you don't mind me asking?"

"I get a free colony of bees. They get a good home."

"Bob keeps bees. He raises honey," said Tom knowledgeably, with the pride of a student who finally knows the right answer. "Right, boss?"

Bob looked at the swarm regretfully. Then he turned back to the crew, more chatty than Ginny had ever seen him. She listened in amazement. It was as if the bees had loosened something in him that was usually wound too tightly for him to speak.

"Mm-hmm," he assented. "You know, that night when you were all talking about what you wanted to do on Fridays? Well, if you would have given me a turn—what *I* like to do—I'd have you come see my apiary. My bee yard, where I keep my hives." He grinned a bit maliciously. "That is, if you really meant it about being risk-takers."

Rosie said with false regret, "Yeah, well sorry about that, boss. Vergina has rules, you know. She said we couldn't do nothin' life-threatening."

"How—ah—dangerous is it?" asked Tom.

Bob shook his head with a low laugh. Tom gave a halfhearted shrug and looked at the others.

"We could go," he said. "Why not?"

Rosie stage-whispered to Tom, "Ass-kisser."

Tom nuzzled up against her, put his hand on her bottom, and stared down into her eyes. "Don't you wish!"

The sun began to dip below the horizon. Dick piped up, "Let's go see the bees next Friday!"

"No," said Bob. "Late afternoon, you don't want to be around the hives. They get cranky. You really should do it in the middle of the day. When it's sunny."

"Why don't we go on Sunday?" said Ginny. "After church?"

"Yeah, right," sneered Harry. "We'll go after church!"

"Not this Sunday. The week after," said Bob.

"Okay," said Ginny, taking on the role of organizer. She looked at the crew. "Does that work for all of you?"

They mumbled a reluctant assent. Nobody really seemed to want to go, but they did not dare protest.

A short time later, back on their bikes in the fading light, they came to the final stretch of their ride. This section of the path adjoined the city and it was one of the areas that the crew would sometimes clean up in the winter months. The path was lit by old-fashioned street lamps with lanterns that gave off flickering light in imitation of gas flames. There were sidewalks, strolling people, and a food truck standing on the edge of a square. Off to one side a man on a bench was playing his guitar with a little cluster of people seated around him. In another corner, on a patch of grass, stood the large statue of a Civil War general on his horse.

Nobody had eaten before they started their trek, and everyone was hungry. Parking their bikes and clamouring around the food truck with its red and white striped awning, the crew purchased food and drinks. As they ate, they milled around in the little square. Bob was suddenly nowhere in sight. Maybe he had gone to the restroom, or maybe he had left for good. One never knew with Bob. Ginny was mildly disappointed, but by this time she was not surprised. She had noticed that wherever she happened to be in the pack of bicyclists, he had always managed to wind up riding on the opposite end. It was as if he were deliberately avoiding her. Despite the winks and knowing glances that Tracy and Beth had given her, Ginny realized that the main emotion she felt about Bob was a sense of frustration.

She shrugged away her thoughts and saw that Tom was eating a hot dog. "Hey, what did one hot dog say to the other?" she said jovially to the crew.

"Stop being such a weenie?" guessed Dick.

"Nope. He said, *'Hi there, Frank!'*" Ginny laughed at her own terrible joke. Nobody else did.

Tom looked down at the hot dog he held in his hand and whimpered, "My bun's broke in half and all, like, soggy."

Ginny, ever the teacher, said in a voice of consolation, "Oh, I'm sure you can ask the woman at the stand to give you another one."

Rubbing his rear end and wincing, Tom said, "No, I mean from bike-ridin' for so long!"

Rosie peered at Ginny's sandwich. "What is *that* crap you're eatin'?"

"A veggie BLT," Ginny replied cheerfully. "They make the bacon out of tofu."

"Yum yum," said Dick sarcastically.

"Hey, what's the best part of a BLT," asked Ginny. "The B, the L, or the T? What makes it?"

Mimicking her, Tom said, "What's the best part of Rosie? The B...?" He pointed at her derriere, and she complied, promptly sticking it out and briefly twerking.

"The L...?" he continued. Rosie lifted one of her legs with her knee bent and dangled it in a sexy way.

"Or the T?" Rosie jutted out her chest proudly.

"What or who makes it is another question," Tom concluded.

"Don't you wish, Tom-Tom!" she cried haughtily, taking a bite out of her hamburger.

Harry drained his cup and threw both it and his sandwich wrapper onto the ground. Then he strode toward the Civil War statue. Pulling a large fluorescent marker from his pocket, he began drawing something on its base.

"Get Harry!" crowed Rosie in delight.

"We got a goddamn artist in our midst!" said Dick, with a salute.

Everyone except Ginny laughed. "Hey, that's not funny, what he's doing!" she said.

"So? Neither was your joke," retorted Rosie.

Ginny frowned. "That's a public statue. He's defacing it. I don't believe this!"

She trotted over to the statue and, as much as he frightened her, confronted Harry.

"What in the world do you think are you doing?!"

Harry continued to draw, ignoring her.

"Harry?—Harry, cut it out!" she said.

"You're not my fuckin' teacher," he snarled.

"That's graffiti! That's illegal!" As she spoke, Ginny reached to take the marker out of his hand.

Harry knocked her away roughly, saying, "Get lost, asshole bitch." She stumbled awkwardly, managing only with difficulty not to fall down.

Suddenly the marker was snatched out of Harry's hand, and Harry found himself being shoved back forcefully. Losing his balance, he fell to the grass. The person who had pushed him down was Bob, who had approached unseen. Harry stared up at him wordlessly. The two glared at one another in a silent test of power. Then Harry rose and sullenly walked away.

"Dinner's over. Time to go back," said Bob, tossing the marker into a trash can and wiping his hands as though they had dirt on them.

It did not take long to finish the trail. The crew rode their bicycles back to the rental shop single file in a glum, tense silence.

CHAPTER SEVENTEEN
Rainy Days

❦

A WEEK LATER

WHEN IT RAINED, as happened often during the following week, the crew remained inside the shed or worked under the picnic shelters in the parks. There was always something for them to do. By the time the next Friday came, it was still raining. They had been assigned to work indoors on that day, stenciling signs and painting shutters. Ginny enjoyed this part of the job, despite the sometimes overwhelming smells of gasoline and oil in the shed.

Bob was at his desk, on the phone. "No, I meant it. I am not going to buy any more flowers from those suppliers," he said stubbornly. "I already told you why. They're full of poison."

Tom looked at the clock. "Break time," he shouted.

Putting down her brush and washing brown paint off her hands at the sink, Ginny went to the shelf, pulled a sealed container out from her backpack and opened it.

"Anybody want some brownies?" she asked.

Dick, who was nearest to her, reached greedily into the container and pulled out two brownies. He bit into the first one appreciatively.

"Hey, they're good! You make these?" he said with his mouth full, wiping the dark crumbs off his freckled face.

"Yes indeedy," smiled Ginny.

She walked over to Bob's desk and proffered the container to him. He was still talking on the phone, his voice rising, and a vein in his neck throbbing visibly. "Because every one of them treats their bedding plants with pesticides, and those pesticides kill bees, that's why," he said. "The only nursery where I could find untreated flowers was out of state."

The brownie container started to tip. "Whoops!" Ginny cried.

Bob reached out and clasped her hand to steady it. His hand lingered momentarily on hers, one finger moving very subtly in what could almost be a caress. Their eyes met. It was a telling glance, one that made her feel a little shiver, but it was swiftly broken when Tom and Rosie shouldered their way to Ginny's side to get at the brownies. Tom grabbed one and immediately crammed it into his mouth. Bob, ending his call, also took a brownie, and then stepped over to the doorframe, peering outside. Rosie pulled a brownie out of the container and inspected it closely.

"You put weed in these, right?" she said.

"Okay, Rosie, remember," said Tom, feigning seriousness. "The secret is to put them in your mouth and gum them without biting down..."

Rosie took a bite of the brownie, looked at him, and chewed deliberately with her mouth wide open.

Ginny then offered the brownies to Harry. "Peace offering?" she said.

Harry scowled, rose, and stomped to another corner of the shed. Ginny returned the container to her backpack with a sigh, and picked up a new paint can. Taking hold of a screwdriver, she tried unsuccessfully to pry off the lid. Tom noticed and ambled over to help her. Together they managed to get the lid off.

She smiled at him. "Why thank you, Tom." She was feeling surprisingly happy and light-hearted despite Harry's rebuff.

Tom saluted her cheerfully. Then Bob turned away from the door and addressed the crew.

"Put the paint away. The rain's stopping. I'm going to need all of you outside to clean up the brush left by the storms," he said.

As Tom put the lid back on the paint can, Ginny, still feeling the connection she'd had with Bob, wandered next to his desk and pointed to the headphones he wore when he rode the lawn mower.

"How soundproof are these?" she asked. "I wonder if I should get some."

He shrugged. "Try them."

Ginny playfully put them over her ears. To her surprise, they were not only the kind of headphones that muffled sound; they also stored music. When she tapped her ear, she heard an orchestra playing

Beethoven's Pastoral Symphony. Removing them, she cocked her head and said in astonishment, "You listen to classical music?"

Bob whirled toward her with a sudden snarl. "You know, I'm getting sick and tired of your condescending attitude."

He exited, and Ginny raised a hand to her face—the same hand he had just seemed to caress. His unexpected comment made her feel as though she had been slapped hard.

CHAPTER EIGHTEEN
Rosie's Turn

FRIDAY NIGHT

THAT NIGHT IT was Rosie's turn to select a place for their after-work gathering. Her choice was a blue-collar bar. It was larger and a shade more upscale than Lefty's. The bar served food, the walls were painted yellow, and neon signs advertising various types of beer hummed throughout the space. A small dance floor, differentiated from the rest of the room by its imitation-wood parquet tiles and lack of tables, was occupied by a handful of couples who, to Ginny, looked drunk, drugged, or both. A scruffy-looking group of men and women, all holding bottles of beer, were gathered around several pool tables in the corner, and country-western music was playing.

Ginny and the crew sat around a table that was next to the dance floor. A cloud of tension had settled over them. To Ginny's surprise, Bob had showed up, but he sat a little apart from the rest of the group, his chair backed into a corner. There was a greasy haze of smoke from the grill, and the rhythms of the music thudded heavily throughout the room, making the legs of the table shake. A waitress with a weathered face and hair that had been died gothic black was serving drinks to the crew.

Shouting to be heard above the music, the waitress said, "...two, three," as she finished placing Dick's usual order of three shot glasses of vodka in front of him. "Who's got the ginger ale?"

Bob lifted his hand slightly and nodded. She stretched across the table to give him his drink. He pulled up a little closer to the table.

"Bloody Mary?" the waitress hollered. "Oh, yeah —for the lady." She started to place the drink in front of Ginny, and then said sarcastically, "You sure about this, now? You're not gonna change your mind on me again and decide you want a margarita, are you?"

"I am not going to change my mind again. I want a Bloody Mary. Thank you," said Ginny firmly, annoyed at the waitress' insolence.

After serving her, the waitress raised her eyebrows disdainfully and walked off with a toss of her head.

Ginny felt uncharacteristically irritable, still reeling from Bob's harsh words earlier in the day. "Someone's not going to get a tip," she muttered.

She stared restlessly around the room and took a long gulp of her Bloody Mary. The music and rank air were bothering her. Although she had started out determined not to say anything about their surroundings, as the alcohol began to enter her system, she couldn't hold it in any longer.

"Don't they have ventilation in the kitchen?" she said crossly, fanning the greasy air in front of her face. "It's so thick in here I can't breathe. People might as well be smoking cigarettes. It wouldn't make any difference."

At that, Harry smirked and said, "Okay then." He pulled out a pack of cigarettes and lit one, taking a drag.

"Do you mind?" said Ginny crossly. "As it is, I'm getting a migraine from all the noise." She took another swallow of her drink, and then smiled sardonically. "On the other hand, if you keep on smoking, maybe they'll throw us out. Now that I think of it that way, please feel free...smoke all you want."

Harry leaned back and deliberately blew out a ring of smoke in her direction. Then he caught Bob's eye and sullenly stubbed out his cigarette.

"Shit," he said in disgust.

As the others bantered in their usual way, Ginny quickly emptied her glass, squirming restlessly in her seat. "You know, Rosie," she said, looking around in annoyance, "this is a bar. Another noisy bar. We said we weren't going to do that, sit in a bar all night."

"Hey, it's my goddamn choice," cried Rosie, "and I choose comin' here. As you put it, '*Sorry, but no. Today it's MY turn.*' Remember?"

"But it's a bar!"

"Yeah," exclaimed Rosie. "A bar where people dance. That's what I choose, dancing. Real dancing, not that crap you dragged us to the other week. Apart from joining the ballet, you got any ideas where we can go dancing where there ain't a bar? Anyways, I don't see you drinking no coffee. Look, what's your problem? Why do you always have to complain? We go along with you when it's your turn."

Ginny signaled the waitress to bring her another drink, and crossed her arms petulantly.

Tom turned to Harry. "Hey, man, I finally streamed that video. Me an' Rosie an' Dick watched it last night."

"Didn't I tell you," said Harry. "Wasn't it cool when they tied that bitch up and started to torture her?"

"That was awesome," agreed Tom.

"Awesome," echoed Dick.

"Told you so," said Harry. "What about the end, though? That sucked."

"It sucked," Tom said.

"It sucked," repeated Dick.

"It sucked super cock," added Rosie.

The waitress put the new drink down in front of Ginny, who took another long gulp and then said peevishly, "Why do they have to play the music so loudly? I can't even hear anything that anybody is saying." Rising and swaying unsteadily, she said, "I'm going to tell them to turn it down."

Rosie grabbed her sleeve and tugged her back, saying, "Sit down. Some of us like it that way. Jesus, what's eating you?"

Tom stuck out his tongue and wiggled it lasciviously.

Ginny sat. "Then you're going to lose your hearing. Know that? You're all going to be deaf."

Tom, pretending to be deaf, shouted, "WHAT DID YOU SAY?"

Everybody laughed but Bob and Ginny.

"Look, I really can't stand this," she said. Her speech was beginning to slur. "Either they turn it down, or I'm going home!"

"Goodbye," sang out Harry, waving his hand.

Bob threw Ginny a look of annoyance, reached into his pocket, and pulled out a sealed bag of ear plugs from work that he pushed across the table to her.

"Oh God, thank you," she said with a sigh, tearing open the package and putting the ear plugs in.

Harry looked at her and, raising his eyebrows, said sarcastically, "Oh—you stayin' now?"

"What did you say?" shouted Ginny.

"He asked if you wanted him to go down on you," said Rosie.

"Like hell I did!" glowered Harry.

Ginny removed one ear plug and shouted, "WHAT?"

Dick rose and clasped two hands over his crotch like a five-year-old. "I gotta pee. Anybody want something from the bar when I come back?"

"Yeah," said Bob. He pulled out his wallet and handed Dick some dollar bills for another ginger ale.

Ginny followed suit. "Okay. Bring me another Bloody Mary," she said. "Leave the change as a tip for the bartender—but not for that waitress. Thanks."

Dick held the bills in his fist and counted on his fingers as he walked away. "Pee, ginger ale, Bloody Mary, tip...pee, ginger ale, Bloody Mary, tip..."

Ginny chugged the drink in front of her, emptying it, and she giggled as she placed her glass down.

"What suddenly cheered you up?" said Tom.

"I just thought of a funny joke," she said, grinning broadly. "Wanna hear it?"

Rosie groaned. "Oh boy, I can hardly wait. Does the punchline go, 'Hi, Frank!'?"

"No. Wait for it," said Ginny with a chuckle, her words slightly slurred. "I'm not very good at telling jokes, but...well here it goes. See, um, these three vampires walk into a bar, and the first vampire goes, 'I vant a pint of blood.' And the second vampire goes, 'I also vant a pint of blood.' And then the third vampire, he says, 'Just give me some plasma.' So the bartender,—this is so funny!—he goes, 'Let me see if I got it right. That'll be two bloods, and one blood light.'"

Ginny continued to giggle. Tom laughed lustily.

"Way to go, Ginny Ale!" he said. "I gotta remember that one!"

Too softly for Ginny to hear over her earplugs, Rosie spoke to the others, imitating an announcer in an infomercial: "The Vergina-o-matic: she complains, she whines, and with a little booze, she even tells bad jokes."

Harry added, also softly, "But she never, never goes home."

Rosie, Harry, and Tom all laughed at that.

"What? What?" cried Ginny, wanting to get in on the fun.

Just then, Dick returned with the drinks, handing them respectively to Ginny and to Bob. "One Bloody Mary. One ginger ale."

"Did you remember to wash your hands after you went pee-pee, Dicky?" said Rosie.

Dick paused and licked his fingers, tasting them quizzically. Smacking his lips, he sat down. "Nope," he said.

"Hey, who wants to dance?" said Rosie. "We came here to dance, right? So—let's fuckin' dance."

She stood and, grabbing their hands successively, hauled Tom, Dick, and Harry to their feet. Then she planted herself in front of Bob, trying to coax him up. Bob firmly shook his head no and remained at the table. Rosie shrugged. Followed by Harry and Dick, she waltzed happily out to the parquet tiles and began to dance. Rosie was not the best dancer in the room, but she knew how to shimmy and to move her hips lasciviously, and many of the men in the room turned to watch her.

Tom, who was still standing next to the table, tugged at Ginny's elbow.

"C'mon, Ginny Ale. Time to shake your bootie." he said.

"WHAT DID YOU SAY?!" she shouted.

Tom grinned and gestured for her to come out on the dance floor. Ginny rose unsteadily, carrying the last remnants of her drink with her, and began dancing with the others, leaving Bob alone in the shadows. For the first few minutes her movements were timid and awkward, but as more alcohol entered her system, she loosened up. Eventually Tom, Dick, Rosie, and Ginny formed a circle on the dance floor, all dancing together. With the help of her third Bloody Mary, Ginny's mood had changed. A song came on that she actually knew, and she sang along boisterously, giggling at nothing in particular.

Meanwhile, Harry had wandered off to the back of the room where he stood engaged in what looked like a flirtatious conversation with a pale, sharp-faced girl. She had a good figure, but her complexion was bad, her skirt was too short, and her poorly bleached hair rose in uncomfortable looking spikes. She was obviously pleased to have Harry's attention. He put his hand on her waist in a possessive way and she in turn began to stroke his tattooed bicep, looking up at him coquettishly. As she chattered, however, he kept turning from her to stare at Ginny, whose dancing was growing increasingly wild and frenetic. Bob was also watching Ginny closely.

After a few minutes of conversation, Harry broke away from the woman. Approaching Ginny on the dance floor, he grasped her arm and pulled her to him, beginning to dance. Even though the music had a fast beat, he danced slowly. Scarcely moving and clutching her tightly—too tightly—he hunched over her. There was a frightening intensity, almost an anger, about the way he moved. Then, to Ginny's relief, a grinning Tom tapped Harry on the shoulder and cut in. With a shrug, Harry returned to the girl in the doorway.

Ginny liked dancing with Tom. He immediately began to act silly, dipping and swaying, his arms flapping, making up crazy steps as he lifted his knees high. She tried to follow suit, and they began imitating one another. Ginny made up in energetic abandon what she lacked in grace. When the music changed, Tom started to gyrate and stepped closer to her, pressing his hips against hers. Rosie, who was dancing with Dick, eyed them jealously. By now Ginny was drunk, and she was oblivious to Tom's arousal. She turned her back to him and, bending forward, laughed as he began to grind furiously into her.

Suddenly Bob appeared at her side and took her by the hand. Ginny, thinking that he wanted to dance with her, began wiggling suggestively in front of him. Scowling, he grimly pulled her away from Tom, who was left alone on the dance floor.

Muttering in disappointing, Tom said, "Find your own fuckin' pussy, man!"

Bob held onto Ginny's hand and dragged her, protesting, through the exit and into the parking lot. His grip was fierce. She tried unsuccessfully to wrestle away from him, and called out drunkenly, "STOP IT! I wanna go back inside. I was having fun!"

Bob moved his hand to her wrist and refused to let go of her. "Give me your keys," he said in a demanding tone of voice.

"NO! I wanna go back inside! I wanna dance some more."

"Ginny—no, you don't," he said firmly. ""Now, give me your keys.

"Know what you are? You're a bully, a big dumb bully. I bet you think I'm incapable of realizing how much I've had to drink, so I need some...some stupid macho guy to tell me what to do. Well, I don't!"

Bob reached for her pocketbook, which hung from a strap over her shoulder, but Ginny refused to let him near it. Seizing her elbow with disgust, he steered her over to his truck and half pushed her up into the passenger seat. Once she was in his truck, her resistance swiftly faded. She took out the ear plugs and sat limply, allowing him to pull the seat belt across her and fasten it. Closing her door firmly, he climbed into the driver's seat, started the engine, and pulled out of the parking lot. There were only a few other cars on the highway, for it was late.

"Where are we going?" she asked. "What about my car?"

"I'm driving you home," he said flatly. "You can get your car tomorrow."

At that, Ginny came alive again and launched into a drunken tirade, accompanied by wildly fluttering hands. "Oh, so you think you know better than I what's good for me? You think you can shove me around, BOSS? Well, you can't. You've got me all wrong! I know perfectly well that I'm a little too...too high to drive myself home. You don't have to kidnap me like this. I'll have you know I'm not the kind of woman who waits for some guy to come and rescue her. I'm all grown-up. I'm...I'm very responsible, and—I'm liberated!"

"What you are is drunk," he said sternly. "Your judgment is impaired."

"Listen, just because you're physically stronger than me, that doesn't give you the right to decide how I'm going to spend my evening! No means no!"

Bob angrily pulled over to the break-down lane on the side of the road and hit the brakes hard. "Fine! You want to go back and spend the night with Tom? Sleep with him? Is that what you want? Or Harry? Or both? I'm not going to argue with a drunk. Get out if you want. But I'm not driving you back there. You'll have to walk."

Ginny began to cry. The alcohol made it easy for her to release the pent-up tears from all of her past weeks of frustration. Soon she was sobbing hard. Bob watched, making no move to comfort her. Finally her tears began to taper off. She fumbled in her pocketbook for a tissue.

"Look, do you want coffee?" he asked as she blew her nose. "And something to eat? You could use some food to sober you up."

"Yeah. Yeah, okay."

Bob drove them to an all-night diner that was a few blocks away. To Ginny's embarrassment, as soon as they entered she had to run unsteadily to the bathroom and throw up. She felt better after that, and found him sitting in a private booth.

Bob had ordered coffee for them and also insisted that Ginny eat a sandwich. She ate, surprised that she was hungry, and the alcohol fogging her mind gradually began to dissipate. It was by now early in the morning, an hour when masks fall off and confidences are exchanged. As she grew more sober, Ginny began to share how some of the things that had gone on at work had affected her.

"I don't understand why you hire people like them. Doesn't it bother you, the way they act?" she asked Bob.

"Sure it does," he said. "I'm aware of what goes on, way more than you think. But if I snipe at them for every little thing, they'll quit. I'm careful about choosing my battles."

"Well, so that you know where I'm coming from, I've come really close to quitting myself. Nobody's ever treated me as badly as they do," Ginny said. "At school and in church and, well, in my real life—oh man, this sounds conceited and I honestly don't mean it that way—but I'm actually pretty well-liked. Respected, you know? Nobody would ever in a million years be rude to me like they are. Those guys are all so...well, even Dick himself said it the other day. He said, 'We're all unemployable losers.'"

"Yeah, that's probably so," Bob replied in agreement, surprising her. "But here's the thing. They get along with each other. I know they're scraps from the bottom of the barrel, but they're a team. That's important. What's more, they're good workers, all of 'em. I don't need brain surgeons. I don't need the top candidates from the employment agency. What I do need are good workers." Bob toyed with the saucer under his coffee cup, and then added softly, "Maybe I know what it's like to be an unemployable loser."

Ginny looked at him in question. He raised his eyes to meet hers.

"Ginny, I was a drunk."

"Yeah, they've mentioned that," she said. After a pause she added, "You know, I almost never drink. Never. But you must think I do. I mean, I had that beer that time and I shouldn't have, and then tonight was..."

"Forget about it."

"How long have you been sober?" she asked.

"Since my wife died, seven years ago," he replied.

"How did she die, if that's not being too nosy?"

A sardonic smile came to Bob's face. "Funny. She was killed by a drunk driver. Not me, but it might as well have been."

The pain that welled up in him was almost tangible. "Oh, Bob, how awful to lose your wife...and in that way," she said. She was starting to understand some of the shields surrounding him.

He sighed. "Well, to be honest, there was no great love between us. Not by the end, anyway. I had made her life hell. I had made my own life hell. Talk about losers. I was a mess. Couldn't read, no education to speak of. Wrecked my marriage. Only thing I had was my job."

"Couldn't read?" said Ginny.

"When I was a kid, I was—what's the word?—dyslexic. Severely. Words and letters looked all inside out and backwards to me. Still do. Back then, they didn't know what the matter was. I was just a black kid who couldn't read. They thought I was stupid. Even the teachers. My nickname all through school was Dummy. The only person who ever stood by me was my mother, and I never gave her reason to. I owe her everything."

"And now she's sick?" asked Ginny.

Bob wiped his mouth with his napkin and crumpled it up. "I don't want to talk about that."

"So tell me," said Ginny, "what would you have done? I mean, if things were different and you didn't have the dyslexia and you weren't an alcoholic and you could have done anything you wanted with your life. What would it be?"

Bob thought for a moment. "Well, I regret the harm I did. I hurt a lot of people along the way, and I've made amends the best I can do. But please understand: I don't regret my journey, not one bit. What would have happened to me if I weren't a drunk? If I could read better? If I had received any kind of decent education? I'd probably be sitting indoors all day in some office shuffling papers, never seeing the sun, suffocating, and earning too much money to dare quit. No, the work I do, being outside, being with nature—that's a gift from God. One I don't deserve. Believe it or not, I love my job, Ginny. You've got to understand that. I wouldn't want to do anything else."

Ginny looked at Bob, trying to comprehend this new information.

"You ready?" he said, half standing.

"Yeah," she replied. "I think I need to get home. I'm sorry, but suddenly I don't feel very well."

The ride home was a blur. She managed to avoid throwing up again until she was alone in her own bathroom. It was embarrassing, especially knowing that Bob had seen her at her worst when they scarcely knew one another. As drunk as she had become, however, she did not forget one word of their conversation.

CHAPTER NINETEEN
Playing Scrabble

❧

THURSDAY

T HE DOORBELL RANG. It was Tracy, holding a large white box containing another hot pizza from Pancho's. After going to the water aerobics class and making a few other feeble attempts at exercising, she had finally given up on her short-lived plan to lose weight. As she came into the living room, Muffin danced excitedly around her.

"I bring food for the weary," she cried. "And their dog."

"Great! I thought you'd never get here," replied Ginny. "I'm famished."

Muffin stared steadfastly at Tracy and eagerly pounced on the few scraps she tossed to him as she and Ginny devoured the pizza and chattered about their lives. After the two friends had finished eating, they set up a Scrabble board on the coffee table and sat down cross-legged on the floor in front of it. With all the food put away, the dog went to a corner where he curled up and fell asleep, snoring softly. His legs periodically jerked as if he were running after something he was doomed never to catch.

Ginny placed letters next to the word *super* to form *supercilious*.

"Bingo!" she called out. "I used all my letters!" She added up her points and then looked woefully at her friend. "You know, Tracy, I haven't gotten drunk like that since we were in college. I was *so* hung over! It was a stupid to drink so much. God knows what he thinks of me now."

"Ah, college," said Tracy. "Remember when we were in our twenties, how annoyed we used to get when guys only wanted us for our bodies? Remember what a pain that used to be—how we hated it?"

"Mm-hmm," agreed Ginny, nodding as she wrote down her score.

"Nowadays," said Tracy, rearranging her letter tiles, "I think 'God, wouldn't it be wonderful to meet a man who wants me *only* for my body?'"

"I should introduce you to the crew. They'll want your body. The guys will be all over you in a second."

"How've they been treating you lately?" said Tracy.

Ginny thought for a moment. "Well, they were very pleased with me for getting drunk that night. They still snicker behind my back, of course, and they make cruel, sarcastic, lewd comments to my face. So I'd say things are generally improving. Some days I actually don't even mind going in to work."

"We won't suppose that Bob-the-Boss has anything to do with that. Has he dared ask you to clean the toilets since that blow-up you had?"

"We rotate with the guys now."

Tracy put letters down on the Scrabble board. "NECK. Double score, and the word "no." Twenty-two juicy points for me."

As Ginny wrote down her score, Tracy said, "So do you think he likes you better now after rescuing you that night? Mr. Bob?"

"I don't know. Maybe," Ginny replied. She toyed with the pen she was holding. "But maybe not. With him it's hard to tell."

"Well, it's no big loss either way, right? You said yourself that he was awfully dumb."

"Did I?"

"But that goes without saying. You like smart guys. You wouldn't exactly expect someone who mows lawns all day to have the brain of a rocket scientist," said Tracy. "Your turn."

Ginny rubbed her forehead, lost in thought, and stared mindlessly at the board.

Tracy looked at her sharply. "It might be easier for you to figure out a word if you drew some tiles, you know," she said.

Ginny, startled, picked seven square tiles from the pile and propped them up in her letter tray.

"So," said Tracy, "are you going out with your new little friends Friday night again?"

"I am," said Ginny. "You know, Fridays are actually starting to be sort of interesting. Provided I don't get drunk," she added, her mouth twisting in a grimace.

"Where are you going to go this time?"

Ginny chuckled in anticipation. "My choice, so it's the symphony concert at the bowl. We're going to have a picnic on the grounds first—you know, the whole shebang. Then on Sunday, we're all going to Bob's house to see his—what does he call it?—his bee colony. It's going to be a big weekend."

"Bees?" said Tracy. "You're kidding me!"

"Not at all. Bob is really into bees," replied Ginny.

"Weird."

"I don't know about that. Actually, it doesn't seem surprising when you start to know him. It fits," mused Ginny. She stared vacantly at Muffin, who was still sound asleep in the corner. "I wonder what it's like, where he lives...."

"Your turn," said Tracy, looking at her carefully.

CHAPTER TWENTY
Picnicking at the Symphony

FRIDAY NIGHT

W HEN GINNY ANNOUNCED to the crew that she was going to take them to the symphony, they grumbled and complained bitterly as usual, but even so, everyone showed up. It was an outdoor concert; she wasn't going to risk taking them to an enclosed space any time soon again. Wide lawns bordered by thick forest led down a hill to banked tiers of seats, which continued to descend steeply to the sheltered concert bowl far below. It was traditional for people to come early and picnic on the grassy slopes before the concert began.

Ginny supplied the food, hoping that having full stomachs might tame the boisterous spirits of the crew. She had selected their picnic spot carefully. It was near the woods on a high edge of the hill where their view of the orchestra—and the orchestra's view of them—was somewhat obstructed. She hoped that not too many others would be drawn to their section, for one could never predict what kind of lewd antics would grab the crew's imagination.

She was relieved that they at least seemed to like the food she had brought. As they finished their meal, they sprawled comfortably on blankets. Several groups of picnickers surrounded them, but they were seated a fair distance away. The crew, at least up to this point, had behaved in a reasonably civil way. Far below, the orchestra members began to file onstage and warm up their instruments.

"This is gonna be boring, I know it," said Rosie with an exaggerated yawn, putting down her plate. "God, I hate this kinda music."

"Get earplugs from the Blob, then. Bob always carries extra earplugs, right Boss?" said Dick.

Rosie stretched out disdainfully on her back on one of the large blankets Ginny had brought, squeezing herself in between Tom and Dick. Bob and Ginny sat on the blanket next to them.

Harry had risen and was dishing himself a second serving of food from the card table that Ginny had set up. He called out, "Who the hell's got the salt?"

Bob reached down and picked up a salt shaker, tossing it to Harry, who caught it deftly and sprinkled salt from it on the remainder of his potato salad.

"Say thank you, Harry," said Rosie.

"Say fuck off, Rosie," he retorted, lowering himself onto the grass to eat.

Rosie smiled. "Okay. Fuck off."

"Well!" smiled Ginny. "Aren't we all full of exuberance and merriment!" She was in her comfort zone at the symphony, and she felt happy.

"I know *I'm* full," piped up Tom.

"Fulla crap," said Rosie.

"I'm stuffed," grinned Tom, patting his crotch.

Rosie looked at him. "Yeah, I always figured you carried a rolled-up sock in your pants."

She suddenly wrinkled her nose and pinched it shut with her fingers, as Tom winced and groaned loudly. "Eeuuw! Who farted?" she cried. "Was it you, Dick?"

"Anybody got a lighter?" said Tom, jumping to his feet. "We'll trace the flames."

Harry waved a lighter in the air and threw it to him. It was the same lighter that Rosie had benevolently bestowed upon him some weeks before. Tom pulled a small aerosol breath spray canister from his pocket, and snatched the lighter.

"Hey, you guys — watch this!" He flicked the lighter and at the same time shot out a jet of breath spray, which burst into flame. "Flamethrower!" he cried.

At that, Ginny stood quickly and reached for a basket of rolls, walking around to offer them to the crew. "Boys and girls," she said, "could we maybe not play with fire, just for tonight?"

Tom dropped back down to the blanket and said, "I come exactly like that, man." He made the sound of a fiery explosion.

Rosie looked over at him and said, "You mean, when you come it's like you farted?"

Tom grabbed Rosie from behind in an erotic wrestle-hold. "Wouldn't you like to find out?" he asked.

She made no attempt to break free, but instead, leaned back onto him. Next to them, Dick, who had been working hard to empty a bottle of vodka, held it up to his eye like a magnifying glass and turned it toward Rosie.

He began to chant. "Rosie, Rosie, show us your..."

Ginny interrupted him by stepping in and thrusting the basket of rolls at him. "Have another roll, Dick."

"Oh, sure. Okay," he said, snatching one. "Uh— what am I s'posed to say, again?" He looked around at the others.

"Fuck you very much," said Harry, his mouth full.

Dick turned to Ginny with a flourish, and said, "Fuck you very much."

Ginny bowed. "And to you, sir."

The crew oohed and tittered at this. Ginny glanced at Bob, who, to her surprise, winked at her. Ginny put down the rolls, went to her backpack, and took out her phone. Moving a little downhill, she focused on the crew.

"Everybody, gather together. Picture time."

The crew obliged, clustering tightly around Bob and posing with stiff smiles.

"Look nice for the camera now. Say cheese," said Ginny.

As the orchestra began tuning their instruments in unison, everyone shouted "cheese" except for Tom, who cried out, "Se-e-x!"

"Hold still for another one," said Ginny. "Fast now, before they start playing!" She took a second photo, but this time the crew mugged for the camera.

"Hey! Who did that?" called Rosie seconds before Ginny took the shot. "Get your hands off my ass!"

When Ginny checked the second picture, it revealed the group positioned as they had been in the first photo, but this time Rosie was holding her bottom and looking around with an angry expression. Harry and Dick, behind her, wore expressions of exaggerated innocence on their faces, while Harry held up his middle finger. A grinning Tom had made devil's horns behind Bob, who was smiling with his eyes shut.

Shaking her head with a laugh, she put the phone down next to her backpack. She was in a good mood. There was something in the air that felt like a new energy forming, something she couldn't quite put her finger on, but the feeling was positive, whatever it was. The conductor, far below, lifted his arms high in the air, ready to begin. Most of the other picnickers had gathered their things and were heading downhill to the rows of seats. Only a few groups had stayed behind on the grass.

"Who grabbed my ass?" repeated Rosie loudly.

In a stage whisper that she meant specifically as a hint for Rosie to lower her voice, Ginny said, "Guys, shhh. The music's starting. Would you all mind helping me move the food off the blankets?"

Harry's way of helping was to pitch a dinner roll at an unsuspecting Tom. He turned away, rubbing his hands in satisfaction. Tom, with a vengeful expression on his face, picked up the roll and threw it back as hard as he could, crying out, "Whoo-hoo!" and striking the back of Harry's head.

"Hey, hey, what are you guys doing?" called out Ginny, trying to keep her voice down.

Ignoring her, the entire crew, except for Bob, began to throw rolls at one another. Bob lay stretched out full-length on the blanket, hands behind his head, oblivious to their antics. Meanwhile, the orchestra had launched into Offenbach's *Can-Can,* a noisy, rollicking number. Ginny was grateful that the concert had started with a loud piece. The music made the crew's antics less noticeable.

"Gotcha!" said Harry, flinging a roll at Rosie.

"Shhh," pleaded Ginny. "Please, guys, no! Not here!"

Ignoring her, a grinning Dick seized a large spoon from a salad bowl, pinned down a struggling Tom, and held the dripping utensil over his face.

"But wait, that's my coleslaw...!" moaned Ginny.

The food fight between the members of the crew escalated. One by one, the few picnickers remaining in their area left in disgust.

To Ginny's distress, Rosie snatched up her phone and began taking photos of the crew. When Tom and Dick saw her doing that, in unspoken agreement, they momentarily halted their food fight, simultaneously turned their backs and started fussing with their pants.

Ginny ran toward Rosie and reached out in desperation. "Gimme that! Stop it! Give me back my phone!"

It didn't work. Dick and Tom had already lowered their pants and were happily mooning the phone camera, to the immense delight of Rosie, who tapped away, taking picture after picture.

"I don't believe you're doing that!" cried Ginny helplessly.

She glanced over at Bob to see what kind of reaction he was having. Bob still lay contentedly on the blanket with his eyes shut and his hands behind his head, completely unconcerned. When she turned back to the crew, she saw that Tom now had possession of her phone and was taking a close-up of Rosie's bare breast.

Ginny continued to struggle for the phone. As the music grew louder, the melee continued. Even Bob finally joined in at the end when he was struck by a roll. His eyes flashed open and he jolted up, grabbing the roll from the blanket and throwing it back with a pitcher's expertise. As the piece of music concluded, the crew fell down one by one, laughing, onto the blankets, their raucous laughter masked by the clapping of the audience.

"I am not cleaning up this mess!" cried Ginny.

Rosie said, "Me, neither! Just 'cause I got a vagin..."

"Shut up, Rosie," interrupted Ginny, unable to suppress a laugh.

There was a swell of applause from the audience below.

BY THE TIME all the food from the fight was cleaned up, it had become dark. After expending their energy so vigorously, the crew seemed more subdued, to Ginny's relief. It was the end of intermission. The conductor had left the stage and the orchestra members were re-tuning their instruments. Dick and Ginny joined Bob on his blanket, while Harry, a little distance away, lay on his stomach on the warm grass, head in his arms, and fell sound asleep.

Meanwhile Tom and Rosie, in some unspoken agreement, began to walk arm and arm into the shadows on the edge of the woods, dragging their blanket behind them.

As they strolled away, Rosie said, "Does it really explode, like, into flames?"

"Wait 'til you see!" said Tom.

When they had disappeared from view, Dick got up unsteadily and veered toward another wooded patch, alternately swigging from a new bottle of vodka and waving goodbye with it.

"See you later. Gotta date," mumbled Dick, patting his bottle.

The conductor returned onstage with a gowned pianist. The latter sat on the bench in front of a grand piano and adjusted its height. Then, accompanied by the orchestra, she began to play a sensuous Rachmaninoff piano concerto. The music, lush and romantic, flooded over the newly calm hillside. Ginny, who was now alone with Bob, lay all the way back on the blanket a bit self-consciously.

"If you lie down, you can see the Milky Way," she said.

Bob, who had been sitting, lowered himself next to her. As the music built, their arms, which were already close, slowly edged toward one another until they were just barely touching. Ginny, hyper-aware of Bob's closeness, was almost afraid to breathe, but she didn't pull away. They lay there like that, motionless, for several minutes, with nothing around them but the swelling music and the sleepy chirps of crickets.

Then Bob moved his little finger ever so slightly and began to caress the side of Ginny's hand. They locked little fingers. She shifted her hand slowly until it lay partially under his. Their movements nearly imperceptible, they gradually began to touch hands, fondling one another's palms and fingers in slow patterns.

The passion of the music mounted. Ginny could hear Bob's breathing become more deliberate and intense. He turned his head toward hers. The message in his eyes was clear. Under the stars, with the pulsing music, she suddenly realized that she had wanted this for a long time. Bob put his arm carefully around her and touched the back of her hair. She duplicated his gesture. Both of them were savoring and absorbing each caress fully. Their faces drew nearer as the music thundered ecstatically.

Just as their lips began to brush tenderly, before the kiss could be consummated, they heard Dick's voice crying out, "I'm gonna be sick!" He crashed drunkenly over them and threw up.

CHAPTER TWENTY-ONE
The Apiary

❦

SUNDAY AFTERNOON

THINKING ABOUT THE unfulfilled kiss, Ginny did not sleep well either that night or the next. She shifted positions restlessly, alternately filled with longing and wondering if what had happened at the concert was a fluke. Bob had helped her carry the picnic things to her car, but their goodbyes to one another were careful and muted, as everyone from the crew had come back by then.

She was exhausted from lack of sleep and skipped church that Sunday morning. When she finally got out of bed, she was full of an apprehensive edgy energy, and she took much more care than usual with her appearance as she showered and dressed. The weather was hot and sunny.

Ginny drove slowly down Bob's street, not trusting her GPS, nervously double-checking the mailbox numbers until she found his house. He lived on the furthest edge of suburbia as it faded into fields and hills. Ginny parked her car on the street and got out, staring at the yard in front of his house in amazement. Instead of the usual manicured lawn, a thick maze of head-high grasses and tall multicolored flowers filled the space around his home, which was a simple, unpretentious ranch house.

Bob came to greet her, walking down a path that wound through the yard. He was accompanied by a large, overly friendly mixed-breed dog. The dog started to jump up enthusiastically on Ginny.

"Mary, get down," he said sternly. "DOWN!— MARY!"

The dog completely ignored him. Ginny laughed and knelt, holding out her hand for the dog to sniff. Mary began to lick her hand eagerly. It didn't bother Ginny, who stroked the dog's silky black and white fur with her other hand. Mary then rolled onto her back and Ginny obligingly began to scratch her belly.

As she did so, she gazed up in wonder around her. The wildflowers and tall grasses, with the light and wind rippling through them, were dazzling.

Noting the surprised look on her face, Bob gestured toward the grasses and said, "It's prairie."

"You have a prairie instead of a lawn?" she asked, looking up at him. "On purpose?"

"It actually takes a lot more work than growing grass," he said. "They're all native plants."

He took her hand, helping her to rise. The touch made her shiver, and he held onto her hand a little longer than he needed to. Then, seeming embarrassed, he pulled away, motioning for her to follow him along the path he'd just come down. It wound through the growth and was only wide enough for one person. They walked single-file amidst the blooms and buzzing insects, followed by a loudly panting Mary, her tail wagging furiously at having made a new friend.

"This is breathtaking," said Ginny. "It's so beautiful—but why? Why prairie?"

"That's the answer," replied Bob, reaching out to stroke some tassels of grass as they walked. "Because it's beautiful. Took me six years to get it in bloom this way."

She stopped to take in the masses of plants surrounding them. The beauty and deep calm she felt came from more than the light and colors. The gentle insect and bird sounds, the variety of textures, the subtle layers of smell, and even more, the vibrant energy emanating from Bob's pocket of prairie wove together in a design that was intense and intoxicating.

He turned to her, more comfortable and talkative alongside his plants than she had ever seen him. "See, Ginny, one day when I was out on the job mowing, it hit me," he said. "God didn't create all this grass just for us to cut down. Grass wants to grow. It's *supposed* to grow. What's unnatural is mowing it." His eyes traveled over the landscape surrounding them.

He paused hesitantly, as if debating whether to continue, and then went on. "I started thinking—

there's so many other different kinds of plants out there for us to enjoy. Thousands of 'em. But we do this crazy thing where we spray and poison everything alive that isn't grass, all because everybody wants a green crewcut in their front yard with no life force in it. Don't make any sense to me."

His words surprised her. She was used to Bob being laid back, even taciturn, but he spoke with a vehemence she had never witnessed in him before.

He looked at her intently to see if she understood.

"Okay, but there's something I don't get," said Ginny. "If you think like that, doesn't it bother you to ride the lawnmower at work all day?"

Bob shrugged and began to walk again. "Compromise," he said. "And I've made a lot of changes at the parks. You've seen them. Wild areas, nature trails, stuff like that. I'm getting the city to stop using those goddamned pesticides and herbicides that kill my bees. So mowing's a compromise. Besides, it beats working indoors in an office."

They had reached the rear of the house where there was a flagstone patio. On it was a single Adirondack chair, along with a bench full of beekeeping equipment. Hanging under the shelter of the eaves above the patio Ginny was surprised to see half a dozen colorful kites in different shapes and sizes.

"You like flying kites?" she asked.

"When I was a kid I did," he replied. "My wife used to hang them up here for decoration, and after she died, I kept the tradition."

"It's been a long time since I've thought about kites," said Ginny, staring up at them.

"Come," he said, grabbing her hand again. He led her away from the house down a dirt path surrounded by raspberry bushes. Ahead of them was more prairie, ending in a clearing with a shed-sized building next to it. Bob stopped, picked a handful of ripe red berries, and handed a few to Ginny. They both put them in their mouths, and their eyes locked as they ate the sweet raspberries.

Caught up in the web and hum of nature, a sweet force once again began to pull them closer. Just as they drew together to kiss, however, they were interrupted by loud thudding beats of music from the cranked-up subwoofer of an approaching car, followed by the slams of car doors and loud whoops. The crew had arrived.

As Bob and Ginny reluctantly drew apart, they heard Dick cry out, "Would'cha look at all these fuckin' weeds?"

Then the crew rounded the corner of the house and came into view. Rosie slapped at a mosquito on her neck.

'Ow! Did anybody bring bug spray?" she said.

Tom quickly pulled out his container of aerosol breath spray and sprayed the air.

"Oh, thanks," grumbled Rosie. "Now the mosquitoes will have fresh minty breath when they bite me. Shit!" She scratched her neck violently.

"He was just givin' you a hickey, Rosie," said Harry.

"She," said Dick authoritatively. "It's girl mosquitoes that bite people."

"Great. I got a lesbo mosquito suckin' on me," said Rosie.

"Oh, baby, baby! Can I watch?!" asked Tom.

Dick, walking on ahead, spotted Bob and Ginny, who had already pulled far apart. "Hey, boss!" he called.

Mary, Bob's dog, bounded happily toward the crew as they approached.

"Here she comes," said Harry loudly. "Watch out, or she'll jump you and bury her nose in your crotch." Glancing at Rosie, he added, "And the dog will, too."

Rosie stuck out her tongue at Harry and rubbed her thumb and forefinger together. Bob walked back to the group with Ginny behind him. He gestured toward a stack of veiled hats, gloves, and white jumpsuits piled on the bench in the patio.

"You can put these on if you want," he said. "The bees are over there." He pointed toward the clearing in the prairie.

Ginny, Rosie, and Tom began to reach for the outfits. Bob showed them how to fasten their veils. Then he picked up a bee smoker and walked toward the apiary.

Harry called after him. "Hey! Ain't you wearing any of this stuff?"

"No," he called back casually. "No need to on this kind of day...unless you're nervous about getting stung."

"Hell," said Harry, "I'm not gonna wear no fuckin' pantsuit if you're not. I ain't afraid of no bees."

"Me neither," said Dick with cheerful bluster.

Dick and Harry both turned to look at Tom, who was in the process of zipping up one of the white bee suits. He stopped and stared back belligerently.

"What?" said Tom.

"Pussy," said Harry, his lips curled with scorn. Dick snorted in amusement.

After Tom and the two women had gotten suited up and veiled, they all walked cautiously toward the apiary to join Bob. There were seven hives that looked like super-elongated bird houses, each over a yard long. The hives were cradled in wooden stands so that they stood chest-high off the ground. The busy activity of the bees as they flew in and out of their entrances created, curiously, a feeling of deep peace. Even the crew seemed to let down their guard and relax.

"Cool. But ain't they supposed to be, like, stacks of boxes?" asked Tom in a wary whisper.

"These are called top-bar hives," replied Bob. "More natural. Healthier for the bees."

The crew hung back as he lit a fire in the bee smoker, which looked like an oddly shaped tin coffeepot with bellows attached. When the bark and dried grasses he'd put inside the smoker began to burn in earnest, he closed the lid and approached the nearest hive.

It was a surreal world, with light layers of smoke spreading out from the smoker and the humming sound of thousands of bees. In addition to the smoky scent, there was another subtler fragrance, a good smell, coming from the hives themselves. Ginny realized that it was familiar; Bob often smelled like that. As if sensing that she was thinking of him, he glanced quickly at her veiled face.

Near the bees stood a cozy, neatly painted white building that looked like a playhouse or a large dollhouse, with green shutters and geranium-filled window planters.

"So is that your meth lab?" asked Tom, pointing at it.

"It's my honey house," explained Bob. "It's where I take the comb from the hives and extract the honey."

For once, no wisecracks emanated from the crew, who were nervous about being around the bees.

Bob took the cedar roof off of one of the hives and set it on the ground next to him. After giving the inside a puff of smoke, he quickly loosened a frame with a crowbar-like tool and pulled it up. An uneven triangle of comb that was thick with honey hung from the wooden bar. It was covered with hundreds of bees. Rosie squealed loudly.

"Shhh. They're not going to hurt you," said Bob softly. "Just don't move suddenly. And if a bee comes near you, don't swat at her."

"Her?" said Rosie.

"Most of the bees are females."

"Like mosquitoes," proclaimed Dick, proud of his knowledge.

The crew cautiously crept forward to look at the bees hanging onto the comb.

"See that big one?" said Bob pointing to a long bee in the center. "We're lucky to spot her. That's the queen, and the others are mostly nurse bees. They take care her and of the young bees. The ones we see outdoors on flowers are actually the older females getting near the end of their life. They have to earn the right to fly and gather nectar."

He replaced the bar carefully inside the hive.

"You mean there ain't any guy bees?" said Tom.

"A few. The males are called drones," replied Bob, "but they don't have stingers. They have only one job, and it's to mate with a queen bee. The drones can't even feed themselves."

"Figures," said Rosie.

"If they manage to mate, they die right away," said Bob. "When the weather gets cold, any drones who are left are dragged out of the hive where they starve to death."

Rosie was about to make another comment when Dick, who was wearing his usual baggy plaid shorts, suddenly began to holler and flail. "Oh shit, oh shit, I feel a bee! A fucking bee just crawled up into my shorts!"

"Quiet down and stop moving!" commanded Bob in a low voice.

Dick did not pay attention. He continued to jump and yell. Suddenly a moth fluttered out from his shorts. Everyone laughed but Harry, who had been backing as far away from the hives as he dared.

"It finally happened," crowed Rosie. "Dick's little weenie turned into a butterfly."

Tom noticed Harry moving away, and called out, "Hey, Harry, I thought you wasn't afraid!"

Harry glowered at him, but before he could answer, Bob said, "Okay, everybody, I'm going to take out some honey. Get ready to run into the honey house before the bees realize what we're doing!"

Bob squirted an extra puff of smoke onto the hive and, putting down the smoker, pulled out another frame that was full of honey. He had a soft brush that he used deftly to brush off most of the bees. He set the frame into a special container and quickly put the long top back on the hive. Then, with the crew laughing and screaming, everybody raced to the honey house and crammed inside. Bob swiftly shut the door.

Golden sunlight filtered through the windows onto rough wooden shelves filled with dozens of amber jars of honey, fragrant beeswax candles, and beekeeping equipment. In the small space, Rosie, Tom, and Ginny removed their veils and stepped out of their bee suits. Bob then demonstrated how to crush the comb to get honey.

After everyone had gotten a taste and made the requisite wisecracks, one by one the crew began to straggle out, licking their fingers as they left.

Dick hesitated for a moment in the doorway and turned back. "Sure you guys don't wanna come with us?" he asked. "We're gonna stop off at Lefty's for a few drinks."

Ginny emphatically shook her head no. Bob, who was folding up the bee veils and stacking them on a shelf, said, "I'm leaving in a minute myself to visit my mother."

"Your loss. So long, then."

Ginny waved goodbye.

"See you guys tomorrow morning," called Rosie, the last to leave.

As they headed back to the street, their fading voices drifted in from outside.

"Hey, look...a butterfly," Tom shouted jubilantly. "D'ya think it's Dick's weenie?"

"Gotta be," said Rosie. "Look how tiny and small it is."

And suddenly, finally, Ginny and Bob were alone together. Bob scooped up a small piece of comb honey with his fingers and offered it to Ginny. She steadied his hand, holding it in hers, and ate the fragrant honey from his fingers.

Suddenly, unstoppably, they came together and kissed. It was a deep kiss, one of tender exploration and long-withheld desire. When they finally pulled apart, they did so with reluctance.

"You have to go see your mother," Ginny murmured.

They kissed again with the urgency of people whose needs have been stifled too long. Bob then began to kiss Ginny's face lightly while she memorized his ears, his cheekbones, his neck, and his shoulders with her fingers.

"You and I," said Bob between kisses. "When?"

Ginny pulled back, smiling. "Are you asking me on a date?"

Bob smiled, still kissing her.

"During the week would be too hard," she said.

Bob nodded, pulling away unwillingly.

"And it's Harry's turn to take us someplace after work on Friday" she continued. "So...next Saturday?"

"Saturday. Six days. I don't know how I'm going to get through the week if I have to be around you every day."

CHAPTER TWENTY-TWO
Back to the Bathrooms

MONDAY MORNING

THE NEXT MORNING, Ginny entered the shed to find that the crew had already arrived. Tom and Dick were each straddling short-handled shovels. Grasping the handles, which arose erect from between their legs, they leaped about the shed, clashing into one another in sword-fight fashion, as Rosie cheered them on. Harry pulled out a rake, put the handle between his legs, and joined in the fray.

Then Bob entered and, like guilty children, they put down their tools and quietly began to change into their overalls. As he went to examine the time cards, he stole a fast glance at Ginny and winked at her.

Then he became business-like. "Guys, I'm gonna need you all this week to help put up the new sports equipment shed," Bob said briskly. "Girls, you're gonna be on your own. I'll need you two to cover the restrooms in the morning." He avoided meeting Ginny's eyes. "In the afternoon, try to do what mowing you can, one park a day. Dick, before you come to the building site, drop them off with the mowers."

"On our own?" said Rosie, perking up. "You gonna sneak around and check on us?"

Bob stared at her sternly. "Maybe. Why?"

Rosie stuck a piece of gum in her mouth and whined, "How come I can't help build the shed?"

"You don't have any carpentry experience, Rosie. Neither does Ginny. The guys do."

Rosie stomped grumpily over to gather up the cleaning equipment as the men prepared to leave. "Motherfuckin' son of a bitch."

"Rosie, Rosie, show us your tit," said Harry in a monotone.

"Kiss my ass," she said wearily.

"C'mon, Rosie," urged Tom. "How about twins? Might be a long time before we get another look."

With a sour expression on her face, Rosie unzipped her coveralls and briefly hauled out both breasts, to the delighted crows and yips of the crew. Bob, with his back to her, did not pay attention.

LATER THAT MORNING, when the women found themselves once again scrubbing restrooms, Ginny, who was on her knees, paused and propped herself against a wall. "Rosie, tell me something.

Why do you do that, show your breast to the guys whenever they ask?"

"Why not?"

"Because it's demeaning."

"Whaddya mean, it's 'mean'?"

"It's degrading. Humiliating."

"I ain't humiliated none," said Rosie defensively. "You're the only one who's got a problem with it."

"But don't you see the inequality? It's all so one-sided. Don't you think that if you're going to reveal something that personal to them, they should show you something personal back?"

Rosie wrinkled her nose. "No thanks," she smirked.

"You don't honestly think they'd actually show you anything, you know, private, if you said something like, *'Tom, Tom, show us your...'* " Ginny stopped.

"...your prick?" said Rosie, completing the sentence. "Are you kiddin'? Those guys? Hell, they'd walk around all day bare-ass with their pants around their ankles if they thought you'd get a buzz from lookin' at 'em."

Rosie entered a stall and closed the door behind her.

"Well, okay, on that account you're probably right. The thing is, Rosie," persisted Ginny, "when they ask you to show your...your 'tit,' they're treating you like an object, not a person."

"Who cares? They enjoy it. It's all right with me to be an object."

"But it's only about turning them on. That's all they value you for."

"I got no problem turning on guys," came the voice from the stall. "I don't hear nobody asking you to show 'em *your* tits." Rosie began to grunt from the toilet stall unselfconsciously.

Ginny made a face and quickly jumped up, moving toward the door to the outside. "Forget it."

CHAPTER TWENTY-THREE
The Dirt Bike

FRIDAY AFTER WORK

G INNY HADN'T SEEN Bob all week after that Monday morning, and she was sure that he had deliberately planned it that way. It had been hard work to keep both her daydreams and her hormones in check. When Friday came, she grew excited about seeing him again. He always showed up for their Friday night gatherings.

It was Harry's turn to choose what they were going to do, and he had printed out maps that he handed wordlessly to the crew at the end of the day. They were going to gather at a remote area outside of town to ride his dirt bike.

Ginny went home to have a quick bite to eat and to take a hurried shower. After changing into shorts and a top that she hoped looked attractive, she got into her car and followed Harry's map, driving to a lonely road not marked on any GPS.

She parked behind a car with an empty trailer behind it. Down a little hill, she spotted the crew milling around Harry and his dirt bike. They stood next to a dust-filled trail that twisted in a loop through some abandoned fields. Ginny hopped out of her car lightly, fighting back a smile of anticipation. She opened the trunk and pulled out a brightly patterned kite. Scanning the group below to see where Bob was, she realized that he was missing. She looked at the vehicles parked at the edge of the road and saw that his truck was not among them. Her heart sank a few notches. Maybe he was running late.

Clutching the kite, she walked down the hill, joining the crew just as Dick climbed onto the dirt bike and revved the engine noisily. Tom hopped on behind him.

"Where's Bob?" she asked, as the two skidded off, whooping loudly.

"He ain't comin'," said Harry with a dismissive shrug. He was watching the bike and the dust cloud it left in its wake.

Ginny's smile faded. Rosie moved closer to Harry and nudged at him with her hip.

"I'm gonna win the pool!" she said confidently.

Harry then looked away from the dirt bike and stared at Ginny's kite. "What's that?" he sneered.

"Well obviously, it's a kite," replied Ginny, trying her best to act chipper. "I thought we could maybe fly it while we're waiting to ride on your bike."

"Jesus, whaddya think we're doing here? Playin' Charlie Brown and Snoopy?" he retorted.

"It's for fun," said Ginny. "I thought…"

Rosie shifted and faced her confrontationally. "It's not your *turn*, Ginny Ale! It's Harry's turn, and he can do whatever he wants."

Ginny bit her lip, nodded, and carried the kite up the hill to her car. On her way back down, she stumbled over a discarded beer can and skinned her knee. Just as she reached the group again, Dick roared up on the dirt bike. He and Tom dismounted.

Tom staggered around bowlegged, holding onto his crotch. "Hit a hole. But who ever said I wanted to have kids?"

Harry then climbed astride the dirt bike and raced away with a noisy squeal, showing off. He roared back and forth, taking obvious risks. The others watched him.

"Shit!" said Tom with admiration. "That guy's gotta have steel nuts!"

"Oh, yeah?" said Rosie, perking up and watching Harry with new interest.

"Hey, you guys," interrupted Dick, "listen to this. I seen this picture from that big NBA game."

"So what, dickeyhead?" said Rosie.

"I'm scrolling," he continued, ignoring her, "and up comes this picture of Brickman. The camera got him right after the ball left his hands for a free throw. I swear to God he was givin' everyone the finger. Swear to God. LOOK!"

He pulled out his phone and the other two crowded in to see. They began to hoot and laugh.

Dick put the phone back into his pocket and mimicked what he had seen in the picture, jumping into the air, pretending to make a shot, and as the ball left his hands, freezing with the middle finger deliberately raised on each hand.

Tom elbowed him. "Look, look...here's a baseball pitcher doin' the same thing!"

Tom pitched an imaginary ball, and extended his middle finger just as he released the ball, holding the pose. "Click!" he cried.

Dick shouted out, "Football. One, two, three, hike!" Leaning forward with bent knees, he passed the football back through his legs, lifting his middle fingers and freezing. "Click," he shouted.

Rosie then joined in. "Diver," she shouted. Holding her hands over her head like someone getting ready to jump off a diving board, she slowly pointed her middle fingers. "Click!"

As Harry raced noisily in the background, the three in turn pantomimed sports poses, always ending with a middle finger being extended. They joyously called out "Click" after each pose. Dick imitated a bowler. Tom acted as if he were jumping hurdles in track and field. Rosie then did an awkward cartwheel, ending by rising to her feet in a final pose like a gymnast with her spine arched, arms extended back, and middle fingers raised.

"Click!" she cried.

"You do one now, Ginny Ale!" cried Dick.

"Hey, yeah," chimed in Rosie jovially. "What's your sport?" She turned to the others in a loud pretend aside, saying, "We definitely know it ain't playing baseball."

Ginny shook her head, unwilling to join in. She was still feeling alienated because of the kite, and that was amplified by her skinned knee and her unhappiness about Bob not showing up.

"C'mon! Do it. It's your turn," said Tom as the three crowded closer to her.

"I don't give people the finger," protested Ginny.

Rosie looked at her in disgust. "Oh, come off it!" she exclaimed. "Do it."

"No. It's rude."

Rosie put her hands on her hips and addressed Ginny, her voice rising in pitch. "You know what? You make me sick. You think you're so much goddam better than us!"

"That isn't true," said Ginny.

"Yes, it is! You got a pole up your ass so big it's a wonder you can shit!"

Just then Harry slid in next to them on the bike, and climbed off. He kept the engine running. "Next."

Under assault, Ginny clenched her jaw and tossed her head, determined to prove herself. "Me. Show me what to do." She climbed onto the bike, and then looked around. "Where's the helmet?"

Harry snorted. "On the shelf in the store."

Already feeling defensive, Ginny was disgruntled by his comment. "I wish you had told me that before I came all the way out here." She started to climb off. "I mean, this is my first time on a motorbike, and no way am I going to ride without...." She suddenly cried out, "*Ow!*" and clamped a hand on her bare thigh. "My leg! I got burned!"

Scrambling the rest of the way off the bike, she inspected her thigh, where the bike had left a visibly nasty burn. "*Ow!* Does anybody have a first aid kit?"

Ignoring her, Rosie jumped onto the motorbike. Unlike Ginny, she had worn jeans. "Gimme a turn! I wanna try!"

In a squeaky voice, Harry said, "Want a helmet?"

"My head's hard enough," she retorted.

At that, Tom made sucking noises and gestured toward his crotch. "Mine, too," he said.

Rosie roared off and the others watched her, cheering her on, with their backs to Ginny.

Tom then turned to the other two men. "Hey, watch this. Boxing. Click!" He then pretended to punch Dick with his middle fingers extended. Dick, with a guffaw, struck back with his hands held in the same way, and soon Harry joined in the fray.

Ignored, Ginny limped back up to her car, slammed the door in frustration, and drove away.

CHAPTER TWENTY-FOUR
Date Night

SATURDAY NIGHT

BOB WAS LATE. As Ginny sat waiting for him, a host of contradictory feelings swirled through her. In a way, it was like being sixteen years old again, yet there was a strange apprehension accompanying her excitement, especially after his failure to show up the night before. If something had gone wrong, however, he'd had the whole day to call.

She smoothed her dress and checked her hair in a mirror. Earlier Ginny had deliberated with Tracy about what to wear and how to accessorize it, despite her limited wardrobe.

"I want to look appealing, but I don't want to seem overly eager," she had said, her brows drawn together,

"Yeah, it would be just *awful* for you to look too seductive," her friend said sarcastically.

"That's a given, Tracy," Ginny had replied. "We're deciding between two—maybe three outfits tops. There is nothing in my closet that could even remotely be defined as seductive."

"Maybe you'd better think about changing that," suggested Tracy with a wink.

Ginny settled on the blue dress that she had worn to the ballet. It was simple and inexpensive, but still flattering.

The living room had finally been straightened up, and gentle classical music was playing in the background. Ginny waited restlessly, her stomach in flurries, while Muffin, with his ears perked, stared up at her with curiosity.

She plunked down on the couch and fiddled idly with a leaf in the flower bouquet that stood in a vase on the coffee table. It was a multi-colored arrangement that she had splurged on just for this night. Then, wondering why Bob hadn't messaged her that he would be late, she jumped up and walked over to the piano, restlessly picking out the tune of the background music that was playing. Every few minutes she checked her phone. As the clock moved forward, to Muffin's delight she absently began throwing a tennis ball for the dog to fetch. When she tired of that, she turned on the TV and began to flip aimlessly through programs, although her apprehension about Bob's lateness made it impossible for her to concentrate.

Suddenly the phone rang. Even though its ringtone had been set to pretty chimes, the sound cut harshly through the air and made her jump. It was Bob.

"Hello?" she said anxiously.

His voice was choked and remote. "Ginny, I'm not going to be able to come over. My mother...." There was a long silence. "See you Monday."

Ginny didn't know what to say. She began to stammer a response, but he had already hung up. Leaning back on the couch, she tried to squelch her disappointment. With a sigh, she started to check her messages again, but almost as quickly put everything down and stopped pretending. It had been a terrible week and a worse weekend. Her leg still hurt from the burn.

It sounded as if Bob's mother was close to death, if it hadn't already happened. She felt a deep resonance with the grief that he must be feeling, but even more so, to her shame, she felt terribly sorry for herself. Ginny began to cry.

CHAPTER TWENTY-FIVE
The Party
~

MONDAY MORNING

THERE WAS NO more news from Bob, and Sunday passed miserably. Ginny rode her bicycle to work the following day, nursing the wistful thought that maybe Bob would show up. After all, he had said, "See you Monday."

Her shoulders sagged as she locked the bike outside the maintenance hut. Earsplitting music, shrieks, and happy howls came from within the building. Even from the outside, Bob's absence was obvious.

She entered the shed to find the crew partying raucously. Rosie had brought her speaker and it was turned up full blast. Tom, Dick, and Harry were yelping joyously, chasing one another maniacally around the shed and spraying each other with opened cans of beer. When they caught one another, they wrestled like little boys. Meanwhile, Rosie was alternately dancing and leaping up into the air hysterically, waving a fistful of dollar bills over her head. Spotting Ginny at the entrance, Rosie ran over to her and shoved the money gleefully under her nose.

"I WON, I WON, I WON, I WON!"

"What's going on?" asked Ginny, moving to the time cards to punch in, even though it was quite evident what was going on. Hoping to make peace after the scene on Friday, she held her rising dismay in check.

Rosie ignored her question. Instead, in her state of happy agitation, she flung herself across Bob's desk and lay on her back, letting the money spill over her chest. Thrashing back and forth in mock convulsions, she jiggled her feet in the air and clutched herself around the throat, gagging.

"Hey, look at me! I'm Bob's mother," she hollered. "Aaarrgghh!"

Tom, Dick, and Harry swarmed noisily to her side.

Dick cried out, "Is she dead? Is she dead yet?"

Rosie continued to twitch.

"Whaddya think, Doc?" Harry asked, poking Tom with his elbow.

Tom mimed putting on a stethoscope. "I dunno. I better check her titties...er, I mean, her heart."

Rosie, eyes closed, giggled and flashed a breast from her tank top just quickly enough for them to have a glance at it. Tom, pretending to be smitten at the sight, fell back dramatically in a fake swoon. Harry, who stood behind him, caught him. Tom lay limply in his arms with his tongue hanging out of one side of his mouth.

Dick repeated his question more loudly. "IS SHE DEAD YET?!!"

"Nah," said Harry, dropping Tom onto the floor with a thud, "but I think the doctor here is."

Rosie thrashed about a little more, and then in a final spasm fell silent.

Dick pumped his fist in the air in celebration. "Yahoo! The witch is dead! She's bonkers! She's finally croaked!"

As Ginny watched in horror, Rosie suddenly jerked her head up and spoke in a slow, wobbly voice, a cross between an old woman and a Halloween ghoul. "Bo-b-b-b-y-y-y-y! I wanna see my boy Blob for one last kiss goodbye! Where's my baby? Where's my Blob?"

She reached upward, beckoning with wiggling fingers. Tom pushed Harry forward. Harry pretended to be slow, sticking a finger into his nose.

"Yes, Ma?" he said. "You wanted me for sumpin'?"

"Bobby baby, give your poor dyin' mama a last kiss," cried Rosie.

Harry leaned over her and Rosie jumped him, wrapping her arms around his neck and pulling him down onto the desk. She wrapped her thighs around his hips and kissed him wildly with an open mouth. He began to thrust at her with his pelvis.

At that, Ginny lost her calm and exploded. She stomped to the speaker and turned off the music. She was red-faced and shaking with rage, more furious than she had ever been in her life.

"STOP IT! What is *wrong* with you people?" she cried.

At her words, they reluctantly ended their game. Harry stood. Rosie sat up on the desk and rolled her eyes contemptuously. There was a tense silence.

Finally Dick spoke cautiously, with the edge of a childlike whine in his voice. "We're just havin' fun, Ginny Ale."

"Yeah," added Tom. "See, what happened is the boss's mother, like, *passed away*." He couldn't restrain himself from snickering. "So he's taking off work for a few days."

"Fuckin' told ya he would," shouted Harry triumphantly. "Was I right, you shitheads, or was I right?"

"We're *free!*" exclaimed Rosie.

Tom looked at Ginny apologetically. "And we was celebrating."

"That much I gathered," she snapped, her voice strung with tension.

"You're not in charge, you know," said Tom defensively, turning away from her and glancing at Harry for approval. "Harry's in charge."

Harry wiped his mouth, still wet from Rosie's kiss, with the back of his hand and stared defiantly at Ginny.

Ginny stared back at him and narrowed her eyes. "How could you?"

"Well, see," leered Harry, "Rosie opens her mouth up and puts it on top of my mouth, and then she sucks on my tongue with her..."

"Oh, shut up! You disgust me!" shouted Ginny.

"You too, asshole bitch," he retorted.

Dick looked placatingly at Ginny. "But we were just havin' fun."

"Yeah," added Tom uncomfortably. "You always make things into such a big deal."

Ginny was still furious. "Big deal? Are you kidding? This *is* a big deal! Don't you have feelings? Any of you? Bob's mother *died*! How can you make fun of that?"

"Why not? We didn't know her," said Rosie with a shrug.

"But Bob is your friend!" persisted Ginny.

"WE DIDN'T FUCKIN' KNOW HER, ALL RIGHT?" screamed Rosie.

Tom, mimicking Ginny, said, *"But Bob is your friend."*

He again sought validation from Harry, who snorted sarcastically, "Friend? Yeah, right!"

Rosie got up off the desk and moved closer to Ginny. "Why does it matter so bad to you what happens to Bob anyway?" she said, jutting her chin out in confrontation. "Oh, I know. I bet you did it with him, didn't you? Huh?"

Ginny flushed and glared at them. "Don't you *dare* turn this into one of your dirty jokes." No one responded. "Bob is hurting. He really loved his mother. Don't you people even care a little?"

They looked away belligerently. There was silence.

"I guess not," she said. "And here I was starting to think you guys were actually human beings. Look, I've tried all summer long to understand you—to be friendly, but I've had it with you. I'm done."

Clamping her jaw tightly, Ginny moved to the lawn mower. "It's time to get to work. Will someone please help me take the mower out and put it on the trailer?"

No one moved.

"Harry, the truck keys?" she demanded. "Please?"

Harry removed a key from a keyring. "When you're done, leave it on the hook with the mower key," he snapped, tossing it to her.

She missed catching the key and it landed on the floor in front of her. As she bent over to retrieve it, Harry sat on the edge of Bob's desk and spoke to the others authoritatively, jingling the remaining keys.

"Here's the way it's gonna be. I'm going to leave the shed unlocked for exactly half an hour in the morning and half an hour in the afternoon, so if you wanna get paid, you'd better show up on time to punch your timecard in and punch out. I ain't gonna do it for you. And I don't want to find no stuff missing neither. Other than that," he said, turning to stare insolently down at Ginny, "I don't give a fuck what you do. It's your goddamn holiday."

With a rowdy cheer, they charged out the door, shoving and pushing one another. Rosie whirled around just before she exited.

"Hey, Vergina," she said. "C'mon, lighten up."

The door slammed and Ginny was left by herself to struggle with the mower.

CHAPTER TWENTY-SIX
Solo

❦

MONDAY AND TUESDAY

WORKING ALONE, GINNY loaded one of the unwieldy mowers onto the truck trailer. It was a surprisingly strenuous task. She then drove cautiously to the nearest park, terrified both by the width of the truck and by the trailer she was hauling behind it. Even though it was an automatic, she had never driven a pickup truck before. Commuters honked at her for creeping so slowly down the road and a few of them angrily cut her off, which frazzled her nerves even more. What kept her going was the thought of helping Bob at such a difficult time.

Once she got on the mower and started cutting the grass, her day grew easier. She used his headphones and listened to his music, which made her feel connected to him. Although she was reluctant to do so, she even took a few minutes to clean the bathrooms so that they were at least decent. It was nasty work, but nobody else was going to do it.

At the end of the day, she was more exhausted and dirty than she had been at any other time during the summer, but she was also, in a strange way, exhilarated. She found that she could actually work fairly efficiently by herself when she didn't have to deal with the constant profanities and antics of the crew.

The mower was supposed to be locked up indoors for the night. It had taken enormous amounts of energy to load it all by herself, however, and she knew that it would be nearly impossible to reverse the process of getting it back into the shed, so she left it outside on the trailer behind the truck, which she parked in its usual space. It was a heavy, industrial-sized mower, carefully strapped down, and the ignition key was kept on a hook in the building, so she doubted that anyone would go to the effort of stealing it.

When Ginny entered the maintenance hut, the crew was there again, smoking cigarettes and pot, drinking beer, listening to loud music, and laughing with hyena-like sounds. She walked straight to her timecard and punched out without speaking to them.

"Summer is nearly over," she thought to herself.

Even though it went against everything she stood for, she was done being courteous.

ON THE FOLLOWING morning she showed up at the shed, dreading to bump into the others. To her relief, she discovered that no one was there. None of the time cards had been punched in yet. Donning her overalls, she passed Bob's desk and lingered for a moment, stroking its worn wooden edge, almost as if hoping to pick up and absorb any stray molecules that he may have left behind. The desk was littered with trash from the crew's partying. Sticking out from underneath an empty potato chip bag was an old pocket-sized portable radio that Bob sometimes carried with him. Out of curiosity, she turned it on. It was tuned to a classical music station, but the music was full of static, with seepages of tinny-sounding rap music leaking through. She turned it off with a sigh.

Taking the keys for the truck from the hook next to the door, along with a bucket, mop, plastic gloves and other cleaning equipment, she walked outside to the parking lot. There she discovered that the truck door had been unlocked and was hanging wide open. A very drunk Dick lay across the front seat, half-asleep, a bottle in his hands. Ignoring him, Ginny resolutely threw the equipment into the back, and debated whether or not to unhitch the trailer, as she wasn't sure if she would have enough time to mow. She decided that it would save energy to leave it on. Then she jostled Dick's shoulder, rousing him. He stumbled out, bewildered, as she climbed tensely into the driver's seat and pulled away.

Going from park to park, Ginny dutifully cleaned all the restrooms. This, she realized, was more necessary after the long weekend than mowing the lawns. In the late afternoon, she arrived at the final park. As she walked past a row of urinals in the men's room, a sudden, loud blast of music overwhelmed her. She moved forward nervously to investigate, leery of what she might find. She did not want to encounter any gangs or drug deals, and her nerves were on high alert, preparing her to run away fast if necessary. At the edge of the corner leading to the stalls was a speaker, the source of the music. Rounding the corner, she saw Tom on the floor in front of her, his pants around his knees, pumping heavily. A grunting Rosie lay underneath him on the tiles. Ginny left quickly, and they did not see her.

CHAPTER TWENTY-SEVEN
The Return

WEDNESDAY

GINNY WAS LATE to work. It had been a frustrating morning. She'd slept poorly. Stumbling out of bed, she had headed for the kitchen, made a cup of coffee, and then, to her exasperation, spilled it all without having gotten even as much as a sip. Before she'd had a chance to mop it up, a bad smell had led her to the back door, where Muffin sat, his head ducked in shame, looking up at her with apologetic eyes.

"Oh no, Muffin! Not today!" His tail began to thump anxiously. "Hey, it's okay, sweetie. You couldn't help it," she said reassuringly, patting him on the head as she opened the door for him to go out into the fenced backyard. Quickly grabbing paper towels to clean up the mess, she muttered, "But God, why today?!"

The morning continued to chip away at her. When she was dressing, a seam in the underarm of her T-shirt ripped. Charging outdoors with just barely enough time to make it to work, she mounted her bicycle only to discover that one of the tires was flat.

Ginny finally arrived at the maintenance shed. She heard Bob's voice before she saw him. He sounded angry. Even so, her heart did a little dance and her feet felt surprisingly lighter as she entered. His back was to the door, and at first he did not notice that she had come in.

"This place is a mess," he was yelling, while the crew looked sullenly at the floor. "It smells like a brewery in here! I've only been gone two days. *Two lousy days*! And you couldn't even be bothered to clean up your garbage?"

There were puddles of beer, cigarette butts, food wrappers, and empty cans strewn across his desk. He angrily swiped it all to the floor.

Ginny began to remove her helmet, and Bob turned to her. Seeing him brought a glad, grateful smile of relief to her face. He did not return her smile.

"You're late," he snapped.

Still smiling, Ginny said, "I'm sorry. My bike...I had a flat tire."

"Yeah, right," he said tersely, turning back to the rest of the crew. "I drove past North Park, I drove past East Park, I drove past the tennis courts, and they all look like hell. The playground's still trashed from the weekend, no one's mowed the grass, the fountains are full of scum, and you guys didn't do one goddamn sliver of work while I was out, did you? You had yourselves a paid holiday, didn't you?"

Ginny spoke up softly. "The South Park lawn has been mowed. And the bathrooms are all..."

Interrupting her, Bob said, "And worse, I find the mower left out on the trailer all night long. Harry, you were in charge. What the hell did you think I left you in charge for? I ought to fire you right now! I ought to fire all of you! You get your sorry, lazy asses down to East Park. Do the toilets, do the playground, do the lawns, do the fountain, do the playing fields, and when you're done there, do the same thing at the other parks. You better get it *all* done today, no matter how long it takes. And don't you *dare* put in for overtime, none of you. If you need me, I'll be picking up the trash at the tennis courts, but I hope you don't need me, because frankly, I don't wanna see any of your faces again."

He stormed angrily toward the door. As he passed Ginny, she looked him in the eye questioningly. He stared back at her coldly, and then exited.

As soon as he was out of sight, Harry slammed his fist against a shelf. "FUCK! He wasn't supposed to come back today!"

By the time they pulled into North Park to start cleanup it was already mid-afternoon, with only half of the parks completed. The crew had settled into a surly silence. Ginny climbed off the truck and headed toward the littered playground as the others dawdled around the truck's trailer, complaining to one another about their unfair treatment. It had begun to drizzle rain and no one else but the crew was in the park. Sheets from a lurid newspaper blew across the deserted playground. There were empty soda bottles and discarded condoms on the merry-go-round platform, and one of the swings dangled, broken. Feeling observed, Ginny whirled around. Bob was driving past slowly. He was staring at her. As soon as she caught his eye, he quickly looked back at the road. She sank dejectedly onto the back of a garishly painted horse on springs, a toddler's ride.

EVENING WAS ALMOST upon them, but there was still more work left to do. Dick had driven Ginny and Rosie back to the hut to pick up some additional rakes and skimmers. Ginny felt both hungry and tired. She didn't see why, after struggling alone for two days, she should be punished with the rest of the crew. On an impulse, she snatched up her time card.

"Rosie," she called as she punched out, "I'm going home now. Tell Bob I got sick."

She didn't stay to see what Rosie's reaction was. Instead, she retrieved her bike and rode home. Later that night she phoned the main office and left a message that she was still sick and wouldn't be coming in the following day.

Then she called Tracy.

"I lied about being sick" she confessed to her friend. "I've never done that in my life before, but I couldn't handle being there one more second. You wouldn't believe how cold he was! He was like a different person."

"It's probably the grief, with his mother dying and all," Tracy pointed out. "Some people freeze up when they're stressed."

"When my mother died, I was full of grief too. But I wasn't mean," replied Ginny.

"Ginny, you and Bob are two very different people," Tracy said.

"That has become quite obvious."

"It's not like you haven't had signs along the way. At least you found out early on what he's really like. Better you should be hurt now than later. I mean, what if you had been dating for five months and *then* something like this happened?"

"Yeah, I guess," sighed Ginny. "But I think he at least owes me an explanation, don't you? It's simply not right for him to cut me off like that without telling me why. He's the one making the decisions about whether we're together or not, and I have to be passive and take whatever he dishes out? That doesn't sit well with me. When he decides that he likes me, I'm there for him. But is he there for me now when I need him? He dumps me, doesn't say why, and I'm supposed to disappear? It's not fair!"

"You're right," responded Tracy. "It's not fair. So confront him."

After a pause, Ginny said, "No. I can't. I don't want to be humiliated again. It's painfully obvious that he's not interested in me, so why should I go to him and make myself the target of more humiliation?"

"Because you have the right to know why."

Ginny thought about that for a long time after hanging up. She finally decided that Tracy was right. She made up her mind to go to Bob's house to meet him after he came home from work the next day. It shouldn't be hard. She would simply approach him and demand that he tell her what was going on. Just the thought of doing so, however, made her stomach feel queasy. Muffin seemed to notice her tension and, getting up from his resting place on the floor, walked over to her and placed his head on her knee.

CHAPTER TWENTY-EIGHT
Stung

❧

THURSDAY

WAITING UNTIL SHE was sure that Bob would be home from work, Ginny drove to his house. The sky was overcast, but the late afternoon sun shone behind the clouds like a fluorescent bulb behind a panel, making it eerily bright when she knocked on his door. A rogue gust of wind sprang up as she stood waiting on his doorstep, ruffling the prairie grasses and making her hair unruly. No one answered, yet Bob's pickup truck was parked in his driveway. She knocked again, this time more insistently. Inside, she heard Mary barking.

It had taken enormous determination for her to go to his house. That courage was faltering now. She closed her eyes and bolstered herself by mentally repeating the mantra that she had been saying all day long, "I have a right to know what's going on. I have a right to know."

When it became obvious that nobody was going to answer the door, Ginny walked along the pathway through the prairie to the back of the house. Another gust of wind approached and made the kites hanging above the patio skitter. In the distance, she saw Bob working in his apiary. He was taking the roof off of a hive. As he set it down on the ground, he looked in her direction and froze. He stood facing her, wearing a veiled hat along with a white bee jacket and gloves. In his hand was the bee smoker, with gray smoke pouring out of the spout.

She walked toward him, her stomach tightening like a clenched fist in her midsection, while he continued to stand motionless. It was impossible to see his face behind the veil, and the escaping smoke from the smoker created a further barrier between them. Ginny forced herself to smile as she approached the apiary.

"Hi! Surprise! It's me," she called, trying to sound light-hearted.

"What are you doing here?" he asked. There was no expression in his voice and no hint of what, if anything, he might be feeling.

"I wanted to talk with you. I wonder if we could go someplace to talk," she said, forcing herself to smile like a young beauty contestant who is watching another girl get crowned as the winner.

He gestured with his head. "I've got a hive open."

Still attempting to be chipper, Ginny said, "Well, it's late in the day, and it's windy. Weren't you the one who said that's not a very good time to be around honeybees?"

"That's why I'm wearing the suit," he said.

"Oh," she replied. She took a few cautious steps back, and then looked at him quizzically.

Avoiding her gaze, he turned his head away from her and moved toward the hive. "What is it that you want? I've got to get back to the bees."

His reply made Ginny feel stunned and helpless, as though she had just touched an exposed wire and gotten shocked. She wanted to double over and sob. Instead, taking a deep breath, she pulled herself up straighter. She spoke briskly, surprising even herself by her firm tone.

"The reason I came by was to tell you that I'm quitting," she said.

It was not what she had expected to say. His chilly response, however, gave her no other option. This was the only way to save what was left of her dignity.

"The summer's almost over. I was going to be leaving soon anyhow." She turned and started to walk away.

"Ginny..." he called after her.

She stopped and looked back expectantly. He had turned to look at her again. Maybe he wanted to talk. Maybe he would apologize. Maybe he would rush to her and take her in his arms, and the whole nightmare would end. There was a long silence. She wished she could see his face.

"Stop by the shed tomorrow morning," he said finally. "You have to sign your time card if you want your last paycheck."

As she registered his statement, a bee stung her on the cheek. Momentarily startled by the pain, she gasped. Bob said nothing and made no move to assist her, turning instead back to his hive. Whirling around, she walked away quickly.

CHAPTER TWENTY-NINE
The Last Friday

❧

FRIDAY MORNING

GINNY RODE UP to the shed on her bicycle and propped it near the door without bothering to lock it. This was going to be a fast in and out. She had been purposefully late to avoid running into Bob or the crew, and she was glad to see that none of them appeared to be around. The park's pickup truck was gone, and there were no other vehicles parked nearby.

It promised to be a torrid day, and the morning was already hot and muggy. Removing her helmet, she entered the unlocked maintenance hut, relieved that she would never have to return there again. The dimly lit shed, with its gray stacks of tools and its smells of solvents and gasoline, was in complete contrast to the colorful, harmonious, light-filled classroom full of sweet music and laughing children that awaited her when the school year began. Despite that, she was surprised to feel an unexpected pang of regret. In a strange way, she realized that she would miss this place.

She pulled out her time card for the last time and signed it. As she put it back in its slot on the wall, Bob entered, his brow furrowed. The couple stared wordlessly at one another for a moment. Bob took a breath and was about to speak when she stalked quickly past him and raced out the door.

Ginny climbed onto her bicycle, her heart pounding, and took off fiercely, not even bothering to put on her helmet. As she pedaled away from Bob and the shed, she tried unsuccessfully to fight off her tears. She was dimly aware of a pounding, crescendoing beat, like that of a frantic pile driver, but her mind was elsewhere. It was music from someone's approaching vehicle.

Suddenly the park's pickup truck, with an inebriated Dick at the wheel and the noisy crew reveling as usual in the back, came swerving around the corner right into her path. There was a ferocious squeal of brakes. Laughter turned into screams as the truck collided with the bicycle. Ginny lay face down on the pavement, unconscious, one contorted arm splayed outward at a horrific angle. Blood began to pool around her as the wheels on her destroyed bicycle continued to spin and the music from the truck played on.

CHAPTER THIRTY

Visitors

A WEEK LATER

GINNY OPENED HER eyes and looked up from her hospital bed to see Tracy and Beth peeking around the doorframe. She had spent most of the week after the accident heavily sedated. This was the first day she was able to have visitors. One of her arms was in a cast that rose over her shoulder. Her swollen face and free arm were full of small cuts and yellowing bruises, and both hands had been heavily bandaged. The other bed in the room was empty.

Ginny did her best to smile through lips that were puffy and purple. "Come on in," she said.

Her two friends stared at her in shock, temporarily wordless.

"Hey, maybe I look like it, but I'm not dead, guys."

Beth feigned relief. "Oh, you're still alive? Good," she quipped, "because you're the one who's the music teacher. I guarantee that you don't want the two of us wailing *Amazing Grace* at your funeral."

Tracy was stunned by the sight of her injured friend. "I'm so sorry. Does it hurt to talk?"

Ginny shook her head no. "How's Muffin?" she asked anxiously.

"He was a little nuts at first," said Tracy. "I've got him at home with me now. He's getting fat. Lots of pizza."

Ginny sighed with relief through her grossly swollen lips.

"You know, women pay plastic surgeons a lot of money to get that bee-stung look on their lips," teased Beth.

"Lucky me," mumbled Ginny.

"You *are* lucky, especially that the concussion wasn't worse," said Tracy, viewing her with concern.

"I know. I could kick myself. I *always* wear my helmet," replied Ginny. She gingerly rubbed her cast with her free arm. "My head doesn't hurt any more, but my arm sure does. Anyway, I guess I'll recover."

"Maybe I should send Jim over in his thong with a margarita and a trashy romance novel," said Beth.

"Better yet, let's send *Bob* over in a thong!" chimed in Tracy. Realizing immediately that this was not the right thing to say, she added awkwardly, "...or not."

Ginny closed her eyes and inhaled sharply. "I don't ever want to see him or think about him again. None of them."

Beth looked down at her watch, and then at Tracy. "Hey, we better get going, or I'll have to mortgage the house to pay for the hospital parking garage."

"Yeah, time to go," said Tracy.

There was a chorus of good-byes as they left. Ginny sighed and closed her eyes, drifting into sleep. The painkillers made her drowsy, and napping meant that she didn't have to think about Bob.

Some time later, she was awakened by a curious faint sniffling sound. Opening her eyes, she saw a shock of red hair. Dick was standing in the doorway. He said nothing, but seeing that she had awakened, he moved slowly to her side. Upon looking down at her battered face, his eyes filled with more tears. He tried to hold them back, desperately wanting not to cry, but in spite of his struggle, a shuddering sob escaped him and the tears began to overflow. He stood motionless by her bed with heaving shoulders, his hands clasped in penitence, and his mouth contorted with weeping.

Finally Ginny reached up with the arm that was not in a cast and proffered her bandaged hand. He looked at her, silently questioning whether he should take it. She nodded. Dick gently clasped her hand in both of his, and continued to cry. The tender moment was interrupted by shouting from the hospital corridor.

A loud voice that belonged to Tom was exclaiming, "No, I'm hung like a bull. A BULL! You ever seen a bull, huh?"

Still unseen, Rosie replied, "No, but I know bullshit when I hear it. Try hung like a little bull *terrier*. You know, one of those teeny yippy things?"

The couple then appeared in the doorway and merrily crowded into Ginny's room. Dick was still crying softly in remorse, and Ginny did not pull her hand away from him.

"Hey there, Ginny Ale!" said Tom cheerfully.

"It's Friday night," chimed in Rosie. "Your turn, Vergina! What are we gonna do?"

"Didn't you say something a while back about taking us to a museum?" said Tom.

Rosie nudged him jovially. "Look at her! She ain't going to no museum like *that!*"

"How come?" he replied. "Ain't they handicapped accessible?"

Ginny blinked, confused. "What...what are you guys doing here?"

"We come to apologize," said Rosie happily. She shoved Dick hard on the shoulder, nearly knocking him off his feet. "Right, Dicky?"

His face wet and red, he could only nod.

"Shit," chimed in Tom. "We were nuts to let Dick take the truck out that morning, him being so drunk and all. We were assholes."

Ginny wasn't going to let them off the hook easily. "Yes, you were. I could've been killed," she said. "I had a serious concussion, you know. And my arm hurts a lot. Broken bones are painful."

Dick began to cry harder at this, his face wracked with genuine regret. Ginny gestured with her head toward the box of tissues on the nightstand, and he grabbed one, blowing his runny nose loudly.

"Yeah, yeah," said Rosie cheerfully, "but guess what? The cops gave Dicky-head a DUI, and took his license away! Plus, they're makin' him go to AA meetings now. Bob is gonna take him. But that ain't so bad. I mean, if you'd gotten killed, they would've put Dicky in jail, and maybe booked us as accessories!"

"I for one am really glad you wasn't killed, 'cause I'm ready for you to give me those voice lessons," said Tom, unable to resist adding with a broad smirk, "...that, or anything else you wanna teach me."

"You guys are incorrigible," said Ginny sternly. Rosie and Tom kept grinning. Finally, Ginny couldn't help herself, and she gave a sudden laugh. "Okay, tell me the truth. Did you come to apologize because you feel sorry for me, or are you here because maybe you like me just a little bit?"

Rosie rolled her eyes. "Since when did we ever feel sorry for anyone who got hurt?"

"Good point," said Ginny.

Rosie left Ginny's side and wandered over to the window to see what was outside.

Tom moved closer to the bed. "Hey, Ginny-Ale, we never had no problem liking you. Hell, we ain't *that* choosy! We like Dick, and look at *him*! It's you who don't like us, not the other way around. You're the one who's always gettin' pissed off."

His comment caught Ginny by surprise. Frowning, she said, "But what about all those times you cursed at me?"

Rosie turned away from the window. "We fuckin' curse at everyone. That don't mean fuckin' nothin'."

Ginny paused to register this information. "So if you guys like me so much, where's Harry?"

"Jesus, get real!" retorted Rosie. "We're talkin' about us, not Harry. Accident or no accident, Harry hates your guts."

At that moment, Harry appeared in the doorway. "Rosie, Rosie, show us your tit," he growled as he entered the room.

Rosie immediately obliged with his request, and pulled a bare breast out of her halter top, flaunting it proudly for all to see, just as a flock of medical students passed by in the corridor. They slowed their pace and stared into the room with astonishment.

Thinking fast, Ginny said loudly, "Thank you for showing me how to do my breast self-exam, Miss Rodriguez."

As the medical students moved on, Tom looked admiringly at Ginny. "Shit!"

Tucking her breast back into her top, Rosie went to sit on the empty hospital bed and bounced on it a few times. "You know, me and the guys were talkin'. We wanna keep on doing Fridays like we did."

Tom nodded. "We had us some cool times."

"So do you want to keep on doing stuff together?" Rosie asked, looking at Ginny.

There was a momentarily silence as Ginny looked from one to the other in astonishment. Shaking her head, she said, "I don't believe you guys." Slowly she began to smile. "Maybe I will. Maybe we can keep on doing Fridays. We'll see."

"Fuckin' awesome," said Tom.

There was a brief silence. For once, the crew were speechless.

Finally Ginny spoke. "Listen, you guys, I'm really glad you came to see me, but you don't want to spend your Friday night in a hospital room. Why don't you all go out someplace and have a drink...." She stopped herself, looking at Dick, and then continued, "...have some food."

Relieved to be dismissed, Rosie hopped off the bed and said, "Yeah, I'm starvin'." She turned to the others. "Wanna go to the burger place?"

There were grunts of assent. Dick gave Ginny's bandaged hand a gentle squeeze goodbye, and then he walked toward the door. "I'll drive!" he said.

"Like fuckin' hell you will," retorted Rosie. She turned to Ginny, "Okay, then, so long. We'll come back to see you maybe tomorrow or sometime."

Tom lingered by the bed. Rosie seized his arm and yanked him toward the corridor. "C'mon!"

"But I wanted to stay to watch Ginny-Ale do her breast self-exam," he protested as she pulled him out the door.

The room was now empty of visitors except for Harry. He stood a few feet from Ginny's bedside, embarrassed and not knowing what to say.

"Well...thanks for coming," said Ginny finally.

"You gonna be all right, then?" he asked.

"Hope so," she replied.

Harry turned to leave.

Ginny called after him, "Hey, Harry, is it true what they said? Do you hate my guts?"

He stopped and turned. "Yeah. Most of the time you're a real pain in the ass." Then, more softly, he said, "But I was startin' to get used to having you around. You know? We had us an interesting summer because of you." Slowly and mechanically he added, "And I'm real sorry we hit you with the truck."

Relieved at having said his piece, Harry grunted and left the room. Ginny closed her eyes, trying to take it all in. When she opened them again, there was a new figure silhouetted in the doorway. It was Bob.

He held a box of raspberries in his hands, and proffered them shyly. "Last of the ever-bearing," he said. Moving tentatively into the room, he crossed to the side of her bed. "Are you in pain?" he asked with concern.

Ginny stared at him for a moment, and then looked away. "No. Yes," she replied, contradicting herself. She added stiffly, "Why are you here?"

"All I can think about is you, Ginny," Bob said awkwardly. "I want to be with you."

"Excuse me?" she replied indignantly. "How can you possibly dare say that to me?"

"I guess you have every right to be angry," he said. He scratched his ear nervously.

Ginny, ready to explode into tears, said, "I guess I do! I don't trust you, and I don't believe you! You humiliated me."

Bob looked down. He didn't reply.

Taking a deep breath, Ginny said, "Okay, let's get really honest here. What turned you off? Why did you get nasty? I want to know what I did."

He raised his eyes to look into hers. "Ginny, my mother died."

"And I would have supported you," she said as a hot tear began to trickle down her cheek. "I felt awful for you. I gave you no reason to be so cruel. And, by the way, I was the *only* person who worked that week. I loaded the lawn mower all alone and I drove the truck myself. I couldn't get the mower off the trailer and back into the shop without help, but there was nobody to help, so that's why you saw it outside. And I was only late on that last day—which is the first time I was *ever* late. It wasn't because I was taking advantage of the fact that you were away. You should know me better than that."

Bob bit his lower lip and gazed toward the window, thinking. After a pause, he said, "I'm not good at analyzing things. There's no easy answer. All I can say is that I'm sorry, really sorry, Ginny. I was messed up. And maybe I didn't want you to see me like that. Messed up."

"Oh. So instead, you messed *me* up."

Bob turned back to her. "I didn't want to look bad in front of you because of the way you're always judging people. Truth? I was afraid. Afraid if you saw me being so screwed up and weak, you'd decide I wasn't good enough for you."

Stung, Ginny said, "You see me like that?"

Bob gave an affirmative shrug. "Sometimes."

The revelation embarrassed her.

"Can I sit down?" he asked, gesturing toward the one chair in the room. She nodded.

After a silence, he pulled his chair nearer to her. "There's nothing I can say to make it right," he said. "I'm not sure you'll understand this, but I've had a whole lot more experience hurting people than being good to them. I hurt my wife, and she's dead, and it's too late. I hurt my mother most of my life. After she died, I got scared." He looked at her intently. "I don't want to hurt anybody ever again."

There was a longer pause. Then he said fervently, "God, I wish I could take this last week back. I know I acted like an idiot, Ginny, and you're right if you don't ever want to have anything to do with me. The worst part is, if you change your mind and grant my wish and let me be with you, I'll probably still keep on being an idiot over and over again, each time in some new way." He put his hands over his face, shaking his head.

Ginny pondered his words. Then she reached over and nudged him with her bandaged hand.

"Well, maybe I was kind of an idiot, too, Bob. I guess we're both part idiot." He lowered his hands. She said softly, "Do you really want to be with me? Because I'd like that."

Bob looked into Ginny's eyes with amazement for a moment. "More than anything," he said.

He leaned in slowly to kiss her. Before touching her lips with his, he said, "May I? Will it hurt?"

She shook her head.

It was a lingering, gentle kiss, with the promise of more to come. As it ended, Bob, still holding the raspberries in one hand, accidentally knocked them all over the bed. Ginny playfully tried to put one into his mouth with the bandaged fingers of her free arm. They began to giggle with relief, and soon they were both laughing hard, feeding one another raspberries.

CHAPTER THIRTY-ONE
Click

◈

TWO WEEKS LATER

THE CREW HAD come back to visit once more, teasing and cajoling Ginny until she finally agreed to continue their Fridays together.

"Of course, it's not like they've reformed or anything," she said to Tracy with a hopeless smile. "When I stopped by the shed to let them know where I decided to take them this Friday, they groaned and cursed and threatened to hate every moment of it."

"Naturally," replied Tracy. "So where are you going?"

"That new art museum," said Ginny.

THE MAIN GALLERY of the small museum was sunny and spacious, filled with an eclectic selection of paintings and sculptures. There were marble floors and high, ornate ceilings with skylights that revealed the pale blues and faint pink blushes of the early evening sky.

It had been a little over a week since Ginny had been released from the hospital, and in a few days she would be returning to school to resume teaching music classes. Her arm was now in a sling; the other bandages had come off and her bruises were healing fast.

And she was with Bob. They would draw together briefly to brush hands, still marveling at the touch of one another. Then, with reluctance, they would break apart to look at different exhibits. The crew wandered about the gallery ogling the statues and paintings, especially those of nudes, and noisily mocking the modern art.

As Ginny was admiring a particularly beautiful sculpture, she heard Tom call out loudly to Rosie, who stood on the other side of the gallery, "Rosie, Rosie, show us..."

There were three other people in the room. Ginny looked frantically back and forth between them and Tom with a panicked expression on her face.

"...that cool painting behind you! You're blockin' my view!"

Tom winked at Ginny. Just as she had regained her composure, she saw Harry standing next to the marble statue of a faun. He pulled out a Sharpie with slow deliberation and stared at her for a moment. Then he strolled over to the museum's guest book to sign his name.

Ginny shook her head and sighed, calling, "Okay, you guys, I give up." Her voice echoed throughout the chamber. "Come over here."

Bob stood near while the crew gathered around her curiously.

"I've got one, but I can't do it for you," she confided with a twinkle in her eye.

"What?" said Rosie. "What the hell are you talking about?"

"Olympics," replied Ginny. "Ice skater spinning. You were playing this game the last time we were together, and I never got my turn."

They looked at her, baffled.

"You know. CLICK," she said.

Dick held up both of his middle fingers and raised his eyebrows in question. Ginny nodded with a wide smile. Bob looked bewildered, but Rosie, Dick and Tom crowed in delight, and even Harry cracked a smile.

"So, Ginny-Ale, fucking show us!" shouted Rosie.

Disapproving faces turned toward them.

In a softer voice, Ginny chided her. "Shhh, Rosie. I can't. My arm's in a cast. And anyway, we're in a public place."

"Does it look like this?" cried Rosie.

She raised her arms over her head as she danced around in small circles like a spinning ice-skater. Dick, Tom, and then Harry joined in. With whoops, they got on their tiptoes and started to spin around a laughing Ginny and a surprised Bob. As they spun, Tom shouted, "Click," and all of them, slowly and triumphantly, raised their middle fingers.

ABOUT THE AUTHOR

Mary Elizabeth (Leach) Raines

MARY ELIZABETH RAINES sold her first works, children's stories, to magazines in 1973. She has been writing books, plays, stories, and non-fiction ever since. *The Secret of Eating*

Raspberries is her second novel.

She has been a prize winner in both the 85th and 86th annual Writer's Digest Writing Competition in the categories of literary-mainstream story and memoir. Several of Mary Elizabeth Raines' plays and screenplays have won awards, including first place with the Wisconsin Communications Council, grand prize winner of the Harris M. Liechti Award, and honorary mention and runner-up with Writer's Digest Stage Play and New Century Screenplay awards.

Hers is the diverse background of most writers, which has included being a piano performance major at the New England Conservatory of Music in Boston, MA, a newspaper reporter, a play director, an aerobics exercise teacher, a switchboard operator, a past-life regressionist, a piano teacher, an actor, a fractal artist, a hypnosis instructor, a court reporter, a church organist, a backyard beekeeper, and a columnist for an international hypnosis magazine.

Mary Elizabeth Raines is honored, as a distant cousin, to swim in the same gene pool as Louisa May Alcott.

OTHER BOOKS YOU MIGHT ENJOY BY MARY ELIZABETH RAINES
Available on Amazon in both printed book and Kindle versions

- UNA
  Publisher: Laughing Cherub Unlimited (June 24, 2011)
  A novel about an older woman's struggle for survival in World War II Germany

- THE MAN IN THE GPS AND OTHER STORIES
  Publisher: Laughing Cherub Unlimited (Nov. 10, 2016)
  A collection of unusual and entertaining short stories.

- THE LAUGHING CHERUB GUIDE TO PAST-LIFE REGRESSION: A HANDBOOK FOR REAL PEOPLE
  Publisher: Laughing Cherub Unlimited (June 24, 2011)
  A book that explains the process of past-life regression.

- HOW TO HELP AND HEAL WITH HYPNOSIS: AN ADVANCED GUIDE TO HYPNOTISM
  Publisher: Laughing Cherub Unlimited (July 21, 2021)
  A guide for learning hypnosis.

Printed in Great Britain
by Amazon

34764388R00130